EERIE ANIMALS

Seven Stories

Weekly Reader Book Club Presents

EERIE ANIMALS

by Donna Hill

Newfield Publications
Middletown, Connecticut

This book is a presentation of Newfield Publications, Inc.
Newfield Publications offers book clubs for children from
preschool through high school. For further information
write to: **Newfield Publications, Inc.,** 4343 Equity Drive,
Columbus, Ohio 43228.

Published by arrangement with Donna Hill.
Originally published by Antheneum Publishers.
Newfield Publications is a federally registered trademark
of Newfield Publications, Inc. Weekly Reader is a federally
registered trademark of Weekly Reader Corporation.

Text © 1983 by Donna Hill
Cover art © 1993 by Newfield Publications, Inc.
Cover Design by David L. Brady

LIBRARY OF CONGRESS CATALOGING IN PUBLICATION DATA

Hill, Donna.
    Eerie animals: seven stories
    SUMMARY: Seven stories of encounters with weird and uncanny
creatures, including a ghostly cat, a mind-reading chihuahua, a
supernatural squirrel, and a phantom horse.
    1. Children's stories, American. 2. Supernatural—Juvenile fiction.
[1. Supernatural—Fiction. 2. Animals—Fiction. 3. Short stories]
I. Title.
PZ7.H549Ee   1983   [Fic]   82-13755
ISBN 0-689-30956-2

For my father, Clarence Henry Hill

CONTENTS

EERIE ANIMALS

Seven Stories

THAT
THING

T'S LATE

BUT I DON'T DARE FALL ASLEEP, SO I'M GOING to tell everything into my cassette recorder, while I have the chance. Whoever finds this, please make sure the sheriff and the fire department listen to it, and the head of biology at state university. It's all true, and if you don't believe me, there will be terrible, bloody disaster.

My name is Evan Kephart. I am twelve years old, and I live at number thirty-seven Woodhaven Lane, the big house on the dead end road.

The trouble started with twenty dollars. I was eating breakfast with my parents when I tried to bring up my favorite subject.

"Evan, I've told you not to pester us about that any longer," my father says from behind his *Wall Street Journal*. "You know that dogs aggravate your mother's allergies."

"And your father's temper," my mother adds from behind her *New York Times*.

My father is a thin blond person in a gray or blue suit and my mother is the same. They would look identical if it weren't for his moustache and her fake eyelashes. I get my yellow hair from them but not my chunky build. Of course I hope to stretch out to lean muscle very soon.

Cora, our cook, maid, housekeeper and everything, goes around the table to refill their cups and stirs in cream for my father and sugar for my mother.

"Now drink that while it's hot," she tells them.

Cora has hair the color of a paper bag and pulls it straight back into an invisible net. She is a hefty woman who can swing the end of a sofa around with one hand while she vacuums with the other. Usually she talks to us more like a housemother than a housekeeper.

Cora's main job is to relieve my parents of every thought and effort around the house, so that my mother can concentrate on her briefs and my father on his dollars in the foreign market.

Cora is my ally in most things, but about pets I'm never sure.

"What about a tyrannosaurus, mother?" I ask. "You're not allergic to those, are you?"

"Anything with fur or feathers," my mother says, eyes flashing down the column of her paper.

"What if I get one without fur or feathers?" Cora laughs.

"We'll think about it," my mother says.

"That's all you ever say! What am I supposed to do all summer? All my friends have gone on vacation already!"

"What about your microscope? Your mini-computer?" Cora says. "Did we buy you that expensive stuff for nothing?"

"I can't be alone in my room all the time! I need company!"

"You'll be going to camp, soon," my mother says.

"Not if I can help it!"

My father puts aside his paper and actually looks at me. "Evan, there's a new pet shop in the mall. Why don't you ride over on your bike and see if they have any interesting little fish?"

"Who ever heard of interesting little fish!"

"Some little fish are interesting," Cora puts in. "Some little fish eat human flesh."

My father reaches for his wallet, pulls out the fatal couple of tens and hands them to me across the table. "If that's not enough, let me know."

I don't have anything else to do in the afternoon, so I ride over to the new pet shop. In the window is a pen with two sleeping puppies buried in shredded newspaper next to a giant philodendrun with a gold ribbon labeled, "congratulations."

Inside, most of the cages for dogs and cats are empty. A few canaries and budgies are chirping and fluttering. A huge black bird with a yellow beak as big as its belly is turning this way and that on its perch, rattling the chain on its leg. Head cocked, it looks at me fiercely out of black eyes circled in yellow. I step aside.

At first I think I'm alone in the place, so I'm startled to realize that a man in a Hawaiian-type sport shirt is standing at the back, beside a carpet-covered cat tree. When he sees that I've noticed him, he comes forward and says in a soft voice, "You needn't be afraid of the toco toucan, my lad. He's quite a gentleman."

The man is not much taller than I am and he has these small rounded features, round chin and cheeks, little lips and nose, like a rubber doll. His hair looks painted on in black by a brush that missed a few strokes. His eyes are the color of weak limeade and the left eye roves while the right stays fixed. I have this feeling that he has been staring at me out of one of those eyes, I didn't know which, ever since

I looked in his shop window. His baby-doll lips shape into a smile. "What would you like, my lad?"

"A dog. But I'm not allowed to have one."

He clucked. "A pity! And I have just the puppy for you. Did you see the Samoyeds in the window?"

"I can't have anything but fish."

He comes closer, wringing his hands with pleasure.

"But I don't want fish," I say, before he can get too excited by the idea of a sale. "Fish are boring."

"Ah, but I have one that won't bore you," he says, with his strange smile.

"I don't see how. You can't play with fish. They don't know you."

"I have one that will know you."

That made me curious. "What kind of fish is it?"

"A rare kind, believe me. I am probably the only one in the world that has them for sale. I have only two for this area, a male and a female." He leans forward and adds, intently, "Only for selected customers."

That sounds like a come on, but I say, "What's the fish called?"

"I don't know that it has a name. You see, I discovered it myself, on one of my trips along the Amazon."

7

Of course I don't believe that. He looks more like an evil baby than a great explorer.

He glances around as though to make sure no one else is lurking and listening in his empty shop and says in a lower voice, "After I found them, I learned how to help them along, shorten the process, as it were."

I begin to wonder if he's right in the head. Maybe he read my thought, because he says, "Perhaps you've heard of me? I'm Doctor Steinthule. Doctor Emil Steinthule."

"You're a doctor?"

"Yes, several times over. But you can call me professor or mister, whichever you prefer."

"Sure. Fine. Okay." Better humor him, I thought.

"Now wouldn't you like to see my little friend?" he murmurs.

"I guess so." I don't know whether I am more curious or nervous, but I follow him to a dark room in back where boxes are piled in a corner and a good-sized tank sits under a strange violet light. The tank has sand and a flat rock half in, half out of the water. In one end of the rock is a slimy, murky little cave. As we're bending over the tank, a fishlike head comes to the mouth of the cave and looks at us. The body glides out. The thing wriggles to the glass and stares

8

first at the doctor professor and then at me, with big, rolling eyes. It is about the size of a peanut, with a stubby shape and the color of dry leather. It seems a small fish for such a big tank.

"Well, our little friend has taken an interest in you," the doctor professor says. He waits for my reaction.

The fish is so ugly that I can't think of anything polite to say. Finally I manage, "It doesn't look unusual."

"I suppose not. Not yet." The doctor professor says to the fish softly, "How are you progressing today, my darling?"

He taps the glass with his plump finger. The fish darts at it furiously, mouth gaping, and bumps its nose against the glass. The doctor laughs and turns to me. In that violet light his face has strange mounds and hollows.

"You haven't told me how you feel about our little friend, have you, my lad? No. But our little friend hides nothing."

He smiles at me and goes on. "Too bad it was the human creature that evolved to the most intelligent level. The human creature is more vicious than any other. I don't complain about that. That's in the very nature of evolution. What I deplore is pretension and deceit! Only the human is guilty of that!"

He rolls his green moveable eye at me. "How much better to have honesty of heart."

He turns back to the fish. "Our little friend here will always show you its true self."

He talks about honesty of heart, but I suspect that honesty of heart is not one of his own qualities.

Now he's musing, watching the fish turn lazily in the water. "It's well along now, as a matter of fact. The equivalent of two hundred million years, I would say."

He turns his baby head this way and that, looking at the fish. "The most interesting part is about to begin. I almost hate to say goodby to you, my darling."

The fish gives him a scornful glance and darts away, stubby tail lashing. The doctor professor smiles. "That's right, be independent."

He straightens and turns to me again. "Can't you see its charm, really? Well, but it will grow on you."

The fish is now gliding along the glass, looking at the professor and then at me. I would almost have said that it knew what was going on. The professor watches the thing with delight. "Notice that it has no jaw."

"What's so unusual about that?" I ask. "There are other fish without jaws. Lampreys, for instance."

I feel rather pleased with myself. Science has always been my best subject.

The doctor professor gives me a glance of appraisal. "Smart lad! But once a lamprey, always a lamprey!" He rolls his moveable eye and grins, as though he's made a rib-tickler. His gruesome smile shows brown, broken teeth.

I start backing out. "Well, thanks for showing me your fish. I got to go now."

He comes after me. "If you're disappointed about the jaw, don't worry. Our little friend will have one, soon enough."

I get as far as the toco toucan, but the doctor professor slips around it and bars my way. "Adopt the little darling, there's a brave lad! Never in your life will you have a more fascinating pet!"

I feel weak-willed while this man has his eye on me, but I struggle. "I don't think I can afford it," I say, inching toward the door.

"Oh, but it's not expensive! Not for you! Not for the lad who appreciates it! How much have you got?"

My hand moves into my pocket. "Twenty dollars."

"Twenty dollars will do nicely!"

"But what about the tank and fish food?"

"Twenty dollars for everything! Even the special lamp!"

He is beginning to act as though the deal is closed, wringing his hands and smiling. "You will find that your new friend requires very little care. Just be sure to give it enough food, a bit more each day, as it progresses."

"But—"

"It will let you know when it's hungry. After the special food is gone, give it meat scraps from the table. Cooked, at first, and then raw. The rawer, the better," he adds, with his strange smile. "Keep the lamp on the tank for twelve hours a day, no more, no less. After your little friend starts to eat meat, it won't need the lamp. But by then the lamp will have burned out, anyway. You see how easy?"

I am watching for my chance to get away. "I can't buy it. I have no way to get it home. I came on my bike."

"No problem! I will deliver it myself!"

I decide to give him the money and escape. If I don't tell him where I live, he won't be able to deliver the thing. He puts the money in his pocket without even looking at it and follows me to the door. "A word of caution! Don't put other fish in with it."

I am already pedaling away when he calls after me, "And never put your fingers in the tank!"

Meal times are about the only chance I have to

talk to my parents, but it's a poor chance even then, because at breakfast they read and at dinner they talk about her day in court and his dollars in the foreign market.

Anyway, at dinner, Cora is dishing out their salad, when she asks me, "Did you buy your fish?"

"I hope not. I mean, I paid for it, but I hope I don't get it."

At that very moment the door chimes softly. I feel my heart jump up and knock me in the ribs.

"But in the Frankfurt exchange—" my father is saying. He breaks off and asks, "Are we expecting anyone, dear?"

"I don't think so. Are we, Cora?" my mother asks.

"Nobody told me if we are," Cora says.

"I'm afraid I am," I tell them.

Cora is already on her way to the door. By the time I get there, she is standing in the hall looking dazed, staggering under the weight of the fish tank and lamp.

After a hasty consultation, we decide to put the thing down in the recreation room, where nobody goes any more. We put it on our shoddy old billiards table and hang up the violet light.

The next morning when I go down, the thing is lashing back and forth. It glares at me as though furious to be kept waiting. It's bigger and looks different. I notice that its fins are now webbed, more like flippers, with little ridges at the tips. It swallows the food in two gulps and comes back for more.

At breakfast, I say, "I'm not sure that thing is a fish."

"That's lovely, dear," my mother says.

Cora stops with the plate of sausages suspended over my father's head. "What do you mean?"

"It might be some kind of tadpole or something. I wish somebody would come down and look at it. Mother? Dad?"

My father nods and my mother says, "Of course, dear."

But after breakfast they are late for their train again, so Cora comes down. The thing whips from me to her, looking us over with bulging, hate-filled eyes.

Cora shudders. "Sure beats all for ugliness."

"What do you think it is?" I ask.

"You're the scientist."

"The pet shop owner was right about one thing. It has grown a jaw already. Isn't that amazing?"

"I guess so, if you say so."

"I wonder which this is, the male or the female."

Cora leans over the tank for a better look, absently resting her hand on the rim. Instantly, the thing lunges up at her fingers. She snatches her hand away. "There's only one thing I can tell you for sure. We don't like each other."

"Same here," I whisper.

The next morning the thing looks even bigger and has grown little claws on the tips of its flippers. More amazing, it can now turn its head. Of course that proves it's not a fish. Only amphibians and higher orders can turn their heads.

I give the thing all the special food that's left, but it comes back for more. Then I remember that when the special food runs out, I'm supposed to give it scraps from the table. I bring it some leftover roast beef. The thing gobbles it down as though starving.

The next day I find the violet light burned out. I don't see the thing at first. I bend to look through the glass and discover that it's out of the water on its rock. It doesn't look like any live thing I ever saw, but reminds me of some beast slithering out of a mud bank, half fish, half land creature, like the prehistoric animals I've seen in books. It's swinging its thick, ugly head from side to side in the rhythm of a caged animal. It stops and fixes on me, head raised, mouth grinning, showing rows of sharp little teeth. It plops into the water and lunges at the scraps of beef I throw in. It takes a few mouthfuls, then spits the meat out, looking at me angrily.

I go up to Cora, who is busy with hot cake batter

for breakfast. "I think it wants raw meat," I tell her, looking in the refrigerator for hamburger. Somehow I feel compelled to give the thing whatever it wants.

The next day, the thing is bigger still. I throw in a wad of hamburger. It eats about half of it, opening its mouth wide. I see that its teeth are getting terribly large for its size.

It pushes away the meat and comes to the edge of the tank and glares at me eye to eye. I can hear its little claws scraping the glass. I remember what the pet shop owner said, "The rawer the better." As though it sent a message to my brain, I understand that the thing wants live food.

"Mother and Dad," I say at breakfast. "You must come down and see that thing!"

My mother is following her own trend of thought, as usual. "Isn't it time to get Evan ready for camp?" she asks Cora.

From that I know they're planning their own vacation. The real reason I go away is so they can go away.

"I can't go to camp," I say. "I have to take care of my pet." Actually, I wouldn't mind going anywhere, just to get away from that thing, but for some reason I'm afraid to leave it.

"Cora will feed your fish," my mother says. "Won't you, Cora?"

"No, I won't," Cora says.

My mother is astonished. "Cora, what are you saying?"

"I wasn't hired to take care of fish."

"This isn't like you at all," my mother says. She sounds deeply grieved. "Surely it wouldn't be that much extra work? Just to sprinkle a little food in the tank?"

"It doesn't like me," Cora says.

"Cora's right," I put in. "Nobody can take care of it but me."

My parents give each other a glance. "What's gotten into you two?" my mother asks.

My father smiles. "Can't you see it's a conspiracy?"

"We'll talk about it later," my mother says, and gets up to look for her briefcase.

By now I am obsessed by the idea that the thing must have live food. From all over the house I can hear its hungry clawing and thrashing. When I can't bear it any longer, I go to the garden and dig up worms. The thing swallows them whole and looks around angrily for more. Worms are not enough.

In a sort of trance, I go to the woods at the end of our street, a place I've known ever since I was little. Trees and bushes grow wild on either side of a rocky stream. Raccoons, rabbits and chipmunks live there, and birds are always singing and twittering. I stand on the bank watching the water bubble over the stones at my feet. The stream is flashing with minnows and other innocent life. Against my will, I catch a young frog.

The thing seems to know I've brought food. It throws itself against the glass in an agony of hunger. I dump in the victim. The frog scrambles about frantically trying to hide, but it's too plump to squeeze into the cave, and when it clambers up on the rock, the thing is out after it in a flash, grabs one leg in its claws and shreds the struggling little creature with its terrible teeth; drooling blood, it gulps down the quivering soft parts, and crunches up the bones.

The thing gives me a look of satisfaction, triumph and threat, and then slips back into the water.

At dinner, I say, "You won't believe this, Mother and Dad."

"Please don't interrupt, Evan," my father says. "How many times must I tell you!"

"But this is important! Please!" I must have sounded desperate, because for once they pay attention.

"That thing. It isn't a fish. And it isn't just growing, it's evolving! It's turning into something terrible! It thinks. It wills. It's evil!"

My parents give me that look, tired of my nonsense. I talk louder, tying to convince them. "It will soon be the size of a rat, and after that, who knows how big and dangerous it will get! The doctor professor says—"

"The doctor professor?" My father smiles, patting his moustache with his napkin.

"The pet shop owner. He discovered the thing. I didn't believe him at first, but now—"

"I suppose you think he's a mad scientist?" my father says. "Planning for his fish to overturn the human race?"

My mother laughs. "Evan, the things you imagine!"

"Dad, I'm afraid of the thing! You must help me kill it!"

They look shocked. My mother says, "Evan, this is going too far."

"Listen to me," my father says. "If you think the shop keeper misrepresented the fish, tell him to take it back."

"He won't. I know he won't."

"If he gives you an argument," my mother says, "tell him that your parents want to remind him that he's just getting started in this community, and he has a reputation to build."

They won't hear any more about it. For the next week they are rushing around shopping, seeing their travel agent and packing for the Canadian Rockies. They give up trying to send me off to camp. They say Cora and I can stay alone until they get back, and then Cora can send us her cousin while she goes on her own vacation. All the while I see the thing turning into a monster and wish I could escape from its weird hold over me.

After my mother and father are gone, I go down to the recreation room to see how the thing is doing, but I don't find it in its tank. All at once I realize that it's out and sitting on the billiards table in a stain of water. It gives me a look like a guilty child and with one great leap plops back into the tank. I hurry and find an old screen to put over the top, with stones to hold it down. The thing watches me from its rock, sulking.

I go up to the kitchen where Cora is rolling out cookie dough and watching her favorite soap opera on her portable television. I sink down at the table and bury my head in my arms. Usually nothing can distract Cora while that soap is on, but this time she says, "All right, what's the matter?"

I don't have the heart to tell her that the thing

got out, so I just say, "I think my father was right. I'd better ask the pet shop man to take it back."

Cora leaves her cookies and even her soap opera to stand by me at the phone. A mechanical voice tells us the number has been disconnected.

I ride to the mall. Just as I expected, the pet shop is empty. Through the glass I see only crumpled newspapers on the floor and the gold ribbon off the philodendrun.

At the men's shirt shop next door I ask what happened.

"Beats me," says the clerk. "Saturday the old man was there with all his birds and stuff, and Monday he was gone."

I ask the woman in the bakery on the other side. She says, "He was a queer one, all right. I'd like to know what happened to him, myself. Why don't you call the real estate office? Use this phone."

She gives me the number. A man tells me there is no forwarding address.

"Do you know if he sold his other little fish?" I ask.

"What?"

"His other little—"

"You some kind of a nut?" I suddenly get the dial tone.

Cora and I always eat in the kitchen when we're

by ourselves and have lots of pizza and ice cream. Tonight, the third night since my parents left, we had seconds of both, and Cora's cookies besides.

Cora doesn't like to talk about that thing while she's eating, but I couldn't keep quiet. "I think that thing is furious, Cora. It knows I want to get rid of it."

"Listen, if you can't give it back, throw it away."

"You mean turn it loose?"

"Yes. Take it down to the woods."

"I'm afraid to!"

"You wanted to kill it. Why should you care what happens to it in the woods?"

"I'm not afraid for *it*," I say. "I'm afraid for everything else. It's twice the size it was two days ago. I've got two big stones holding the screen down, and I'm not sure that's enough. It's almost too big for the tank now."

She knows what I mean, and we both shudder.

"I thought of another way," I tell her. "I'm not going to feed it any longer. I didn't feed it today."

We're sitting in the kitchen where it's warm and smells good and the clock is ticking merrily on, but Cora shivers and I feel stiff with cold.

We stay up late to watch a movie. I imagine I can hear the thing down in the recreation room, clawing at its tank, scraping at the screen. By now it must be ravenous. I almost feel sorry for it.

We keep telling each other that we're not tired, but we are yawning and struggling to keep our eyes open. The truth is, we're afraid to go to bed. At last Cora says, "This is silly."

She turns off the television and has just put her finger on the light switch when we hear a crash. We grab hands, breathing hard.

"We have to go see," Cora finally says. We creep down to the recreation room. I turn on the light. The fish tank is turned over on the floor in a flood of water. A window is broken. The thing has escaped.

We mop up fast and go back upstairs. Cora walks me to my room.

"Listen," I say, "I don't mean to sound nervous or anything, but I think we'd better lock our doors. Who knows how big it is by now?"

Cora tries to sound natural. "Tomorrow we'll call the authorities."

"Who would believe us?"

"We'll keep trying until somebody does. The sheriff, the fire department, the town council."

When she left, I not only locked my door, but I pushed my bureau in front of it. Then I sat here at my desk with this cassette recorder to tell the story. I'm feeling pretty tired now, so I'm going to lie down with my baseball bat ready.

I'm back. Listen! Hear that shriek? That's the

neighbor's collie. He was barking a long time, loud and angry, but suddenly his bark has turned into this horrible noise.

He's stopped! I'm going to ask Cora to call somebody right now!

Here I am again. We called the fire department. Cora says she's not sure they believed her.

You had better look for the dog's body, but I don't think you'll find much.

All I can say is, catch that thing! It's loose in the neighborhood. And there's another one, too: one is male and the other female. But most important, find Doctor-Professor Steinthule and his new pet shop, with his little darlings for adoption.

Listen! A window crashed downstairs. Hear that slithering, flopping sound? A heavy body crawling up the steps. The scratch of claws along the hall!

I don't hear the fire truck yet. I have to shut this off, now. I'm going to stand by the door with my bat. I hope you find this tape!

GHOST CAT

T WAS

GROWING SO DARK THAT FILMORE HAD TO stop reading; but as soon as he put his book down, he began to notice the loneliness again.

His mother had been driving without a word ever since they had turned onto this remote and bumpy road. Jodi was asleep, curled up in back with her stuffed animal friend. There was nothing to see out the window except black trees and shrubs along the roadside thrashing in the wind. To the west, through the trees, he could see that the sun had melted onto the horizon, but to the east the sky looked dark and bruised.

Suddenly his mother said, "That must be the house." She stopped the car.

Jodi sat up. "Are we here?" Jodi always awoke at once, alert and happy. She did not seem to know what loneliness and sorrow were. Jodi had glossy black curls and eyes like agates. She was little for her six years, but sturdy and fearless, as even Filmore would admit, but only to himself. To others, sometimes as a compliment, he said she was daft.

"You two wait here while I take a look," said their mother.

Filmore watched their mother walk along the path between the swaying, overgrown bushes. She looked small, walking alone, not much taller than his sister, in fact. Filmore whispered, "Jodi, don't you wish Daddy were here with us?"

Jodi was brushing down the apron of her animal friend.

"Remember last summer with Daddy?" Filmore said. "The beach, how broad and clean and dazzling it was? Remember what fun we had in the boat?"

Jodi turned her animal friend about, inspecting her from all sides.

"Here comes mother," Filmore said. "Let's not remind her of Daddy." But he needn't have warned Jodi. She seemed not to have heard a word.

"This is it," their mother said. "Help me with the bags, please, Filmore."

He and Jodi scrambled out of the car.

"Wait, wait!" Jodi called. "I dropped Mrs. Tiggy-winkle! Don't worry, Mrs. Tiggy-winkle! We'll never leave you! We love you!"

"What does she care," Filmore protested. For

some reason he was annoyed with his sister. "She's only a stuffed hedgehog."

"She is not! She's a raccoon!"

"Listen, either she's a hedgehog or she's not Mrs. Tiggy-winkle!"

"Filmore, please," their mother said, pushing through the creaking gate.

A stone path led to a cottage perched on a little bluff overlooking the cove. Trees were sighing and moaning over the roof, and shrubs whispered at the door. The wind dropped suddenly as though the house were holding its breath, and Filmore could hear the push of waves up the beach and their scraping retreat over pebbles and shells.

His mother paused at the stoop to search through her bag for the key. Now Filmore could see scaling paint, shutters hanging loose and windows opaque with dust. "What a dump!" he muttered.

When he saw his mother's face, he was sorry. His mother had gone back to teaching and labored to keep up their home; no one knew better than Filmore how hard it had been.

"The agent told us we'd have to take it as is," she said. "That's how we can afford it." She found the key, but could hardly shove the door open for sand that had sucked up against it.

"We came for the beach, anyway," Filmore

said. "Who cares about the house! I wouldn't care if it was haunted!"

"Oh, I love the haunted house!" Jodi cried, bursting into the front room. "Oh, we have a big window with the whole black sky in it! Oh, and a fireplace! And rocking chairs!" The floor squealed under her feet as she ran around excitedly. "And here's the kitchen, with a black monster stove!"

Their mother laughed. She had the same dark curly hair, the same eyes as Jodi, and when she laughed, she did not look much older. "It's charming, really. Just needs a little work. But first we need some sleep."

They climbed narrow stairs and opened creaking doors to three small rooms with beds under dust covers. The covers pleased their mother and made Jodi laugh. "Ghosts and more ghosts!" she cried.

In his unfamiliar little room above the kitchen, Filmore kept waking in the night to whistles, squeals and thumps that could have been ghosts in the house, that could have been anything sinister at all.

The next morning, Filmore woke to the melancholy crying of gulls. When he heard Jodi's light voice below, he pulled his clothes on hurriedly and went down to the kitchen.

"Good morning, dear," his mother said from the

stove, where she was already cooking breakfast. "Did you sleep well?"

"I didn't sleep at all," Jodi put in cheerfully. "Neither did Mrs. Tiggy-winkle. We stayed awake all night and listened to the haunted house."

Filmore did not want to admit his own feelings. "You're daft!"

"Something is here, you know," Jodi insisted. "Something besides us!"

"And I know what it is." Their mother laughed. "Sand! We'll get rid of it right now."

The house was so small that sweeping and dusting upstairs and down did not take long, and still there was time for the beach before lunch.

To Filmore, the beach was even more disappointing than the house. It was narrow and deserted, with low, dispirited waves the color of mud as far as the eye could see. There were no houses in sight, just cliffs and scraggy pine trees at each end of the cove. Edging the sand were patches of weeds and damp brown rags of algae that smelled like vinegar. The stain that marked high tide was littered with broken shells, sticks like bones and here and there a dead fish. A troupe of sandpipers ran up the beach and back, as though frantic to escape.

Jodi loved everything. She made up a joyful

beach song as she built a sand dragon and then she pressed Filmore to go with her while she filled her bucket with shells and treasures.

Stumping along at her heels, Filmore demanded, "Why don't you ever talk about Daddy? You were his dear rabbit, don't forget!"

"Look, Filmore!" Jodi cried. "I found a sand dollar!"

After lunch, they drove out for supplies. "It will be fun to see the village and the shops," their mother said.

The village turned out to be only a few houses scattered along the road, and on the beach, one rowboat upside down beside a shack with a sign for bait. The shops were only Judson's General Store and Judson's Gas Station.

A bell jangled as they went into the store. It was dim and cluttered and smelled of dusty bolts of cloth and strong cheese. Behind the counter stood a tall, thin woman who kept her hands in her apron pockets while she looked them over with stern interest.

"Good morning!" their mother said. "I'm Mrs. Coyne. This is my son Filmore and my daughter Jodi. We've rented the Hogarth place."

"Heard you did," said the storekeeper.

"We need milk and a few groceries. Also lumber and nails, if you have them. We'd like to mend the front stoop. You don't think the owner would mind, do you?"

"Not likely. He hasn't seen the place in years. But I'd wait if I were you. See if you like it there, first."

"Don't you think we'll like it?" Filmore asked.

"Been a lot of folks in and out the Hogarth place. City folks, mostly. Like you. They never stay long."

"Because it's run-down, or is there something else?" Filmore asked.

His mother interposed. "Do you happen to know if the chimney works?"

"Did once. Likely needs sweeping."

"Is there someone who might do it for us?"

"Mr. Judson. My husband. He can fix the front stoop, too, if you want. Rehang those shutters. Trim the bushes. You would have to pay, though. The real estate agency won't. Cost you twenty dollars."

"That would be just fine!"

When Mrs. Judson was adding up the prices on a paper bag, Filmore asked, "Why don't people stay long at Hogarth's?"

Mrs. Judson was busy checking her figures.

"Because of what's there besides us," Jodi said. "Isn't that right, Mrs. Judson?"

Their mother looked at Mrs. Judson with a smile, but Mrs. Judson was busy packing groceries.

"But we like it, Mrs. Tiggy-winkle and I. It sounds so beautiful and sad. Especially the little bell."

"What little bell?" Filmore asked.

"Didn't you hear it? It was so sweet last night, going tinkle-clink all around the house."

Mrs. Judson rang up the money with a loud jangle of her register. "Suit you if Mr. Judson comes tomorrow morning?"

Back in the car, Filmore said, "She wasn't very friendly."

"I thought she was," said their mother. "She tried to help us all she could."

"She didn't smile, not once," Filmore said. "And she wouldn't tell us anything."

"That's because she was nervous," Jodi said.

"Why would she be nervous?" their mother asked.

"For us. She thinks we might be afraid in the house."

"But there's nothing to be afraid of!" said their mother.

Jodi laughed. "We know that!"

Early next morning, Mr. Judson arrived in a truck, with toolbox and planks of wood. He too was tall and thin, with the same gaunt face as his wife, but with a tuft of gray beard attached.

All morning while they were on the beach, Filmore could hear Mr. Judson hammering, thumping and snipping. At noon he came and said, "Chimney's working. I laid a fire. Got to go, now. The missus will be waiting."

They walked with him to his truck. "How do you folks like it here?" he asked, lifting his toolbox into the back.

"We love it!" Jodi answered.

"It's a charming house, really," their mother said. "I wonder why it hasn't been sold?"

"Because of what's here," Jodi said. "Isn't that right, Mr. Judson?"

Mr. Judson was searching among his tools. "Must have left my pliers somewhere, Mrs. Coyne."

"It's a cat," Jodi said.

"A cat, Jodi?" their mother asked. "Are you sure? Is there a cat, Mr. Judson?"

"Never saw one here, myself. Leastwise not in years."

"You mean there used to be a cat?" Filmore asked.

"Mrs. Hogarth, she had one. Hogarth, he moved away when his missus died. Don't know what became of the cat."

"Could it be a neighbor's cat?"

"She has a squeaky little voice," Jodi said. "Probably hoarse from crying."

"Haven't heard tell of any lost cats," Mr. Judson said. He went around to the cab of his truck.

"Could it be a stray?"

"Oh, she's not a stray," Jodi said. "She wears a little rusty bell that goes tinkle-clink when she runs. It's so sweet."

Mr. Judson climbed into his truck and turned on the ignition. "If you find my pliers, will you bring them next time?"

As they watched the truck rattle down the road, Filmore asked, "Don't you think the Judsons act strange? Like they're hiding something?"

"No, dear," his mother said. "I think they're just reticent. That's how people are in this part of the country."

That night, Filmore was awakened by someone shaking his toes. "Filmore! I have to tell you something!"

Jodi was leaning against his bed with Mrs. Tiggy-winkle in her arms. Moonlight falling through the window made her eyes like holes in a mask. "Do you hear the cat?" Jodi whispered. "She's prowling and crying all around the house, now. She wants to come in."

Filmore held his breath to listen. He did in fact hear a wailing and sighing and rustling of leaves. "That's the wind."

"And the cat, too," Jodi insisted.

"All right, get in my bed, if you're scared."

"We're not scared. But we are cold." She climbed on the bed and settled the quilt around Mrs. Tiggy-winkle.

Filmore rolled over and closed his eyes. "Go to sleep. There isn't any cat. Mr. Judson said so."

"He did not. He said he never saw a cat, least-wise not in years. But we did."

Filmore turned back. "You saw it?"

"Yes, on the beach this afternoon. She was watching us through the weeds, a yellow cat with red eyes."

"Then why haven't mother and I seen it?"

"Because she's invisible."

"You said you saw it!"

"We did! Mrs. Tiggy-winkle and I! Both of us! First we saw her eyes and then we saw her whole self!"

"You don't even know what invisible means!"

"We do too! It means mostly people can't see her."

"It means nobody ever sees her!"

"But she can fix that when she wants to. Any-way, she is prowling and crying right now. She wants somebody to let her in."

"If she's invisible, she can let herself in!" Filmore cried, triumphantly.

"That's not the same," Jodi said, straightening the quilt.

Filmore turned away. "You make me tired! What did you come bothering me for!"

Jodi sighed and threw off the covers.

"You can stay if you're nervous," Filmore muttered.

"We aren't nervous. But you are! So we'll stay."

At breakfast, Jodi said, through a mouthful of blueberry pancakes, "When you have a cat, you're her mother and daddy, you know, so you must never leave her, like Mr. Hogarth did. That's why she's always crying and prowling and never can rest."

Their mother looked down at them from her pancake griddle.

"We have to put some food out for her, Mother," Jodi said.

"If there's any cat around here, it finds its own food," Filmore said.

"That's right, dear. It got along all right before we came."

"No, she didn't! She's skinny all over and her little bones show! Can't I give her my milk? Please, Mother, please!"

Their mother smiled. "Not your milk, Jodi. We'll find some scraps."

Filmore followed Jodi to the kitchen stoop, where she settled the scraps and a pan of water.

"She's already been here, looking for food," Jodi said. "See her paw prints?"

Filmore bent to examine the stoop. "That's just wet sand. The wind did that. You're putting this food here for nothing. No cat's going to eat it."

"Of course not. She's a ghost. Ghosts can't eat."

"Then why are you putting it here!" Filmore exclaimed, exasperated.

"She doesn't need to eat it, just to have it. To know we love her."

On the beach that afternoon, their mother was reading under the umbrella while Jodi sat beside her on the sand, sorting her beach treasure. Filmore waded for a while, but he felt uneasy by himself and soon came back to flop beside his sister.

The grasses above the beach rattled in the wind. "Is the cat watching us now?" he whispered.

"Oh, not now. The hot sand hurts her feet."

"I thought you said she was ghost!"

"But she can hurt, just the same."

Later, clouds rolled up over the sea and the wind turned cold. Filmore took down the umbrella while his mother folded the beach chair and they ran for the house through pellets of rain.

That evening Filmore forgot the cat in the pleasure of popping corn over a snappy fire. Their mother sat rocking and mending, and Jodi sprawled on the hearth, humming to Mrs. Tiggy-winkle. Fire-light threw quivering shadows on the walls. Outside the rain was like handfuls of sand thrown at the windows.

Filmore glanced at his mother. Her face was thoughtful and withdrawn. Whenever he caught her in such a mood, she would quickly smile, as though to insist she was all right. This time, however, she spoke.

"Remember last summer? Our last vacation with Daddy? Remember the day he bought every balloon the man had, and you three went along the beach and gave them away to children? He wanted us to share our happiness. Remember, Jodi, how happy he wanted us to be?"

"Is it popcorn yet?" Jodi asked. "I don't hear any more pops."

When Filmore passed her the popcorn, she said, "Mrs. Tiggy-winkle feels just the same as me. But not the cat. She hurts. Because she was murdered. That's why she's a ghost."

Filmore saw that his mother's needle had stopped, but she did not look at them.

"When somebody leaves you, they always murder you a little bit. But Mr. Hogarth, he murdered her a lot, until she was dead."

"If you know so much, how did he do it?" Filmore demanded.

"First he starved her and then he drowned her and then he told her she was bad. That's why she's so skinny and wet. She hates to be skinny and wet. She's outside now, crying at the kitchen door. Can't you hear her? She wants to come in by the fire."

"You're daft!" Filmore exclaimed. "That's just the wind!"

"Please, Mother, please! Can't I let her in?"

Their mother gave Filmore a glance that asked for patience. "All right, dear. Let her in."

Jodi rose with Mrs. Tiggy-winkle and went to the kitchen. Filmore heard the kitchen door open and then the screen. A cold draft blew through the room and dashed at the flames on the hearth.

"Hurry up, please!" their mother called. "You're cooling off the house."

When Jodi came back, Filmore said, "Well, where is the cat?"

"She can't come in because she knows you don't love her."

"But you and Mrs. Tiggy-winkle love her! Isn't that enough?"

"Can Mrs. Tiggy-winkle have some more popcorn, please?"

When the fire burned low and their mother announced bedtime, Jodi said, "She's crying again, Mother."

"Jodi, dear, why do you upset yourself this way? Can't you just enjoy your vacation with Filmore and me?"

"Yes, but she has to be happy, too! That's why we came here, you know! Can't I let her sleep on my bed tonight?"

Their mother sighed.

"You think I just imagine her, don't you?"

"Of course!" Filmore said. "You are the only one who sees her!"

"I am not! Mrs. Tiggy-winkle sees her, too!"

"And Mrs. Tiggy-winkle isn't real, either!"

"All right, if I just imagine her, why can't I have her on my bed?"

Their mother smiled. "I can't argue with that."

In his room, Filmore heard the squeal and slap of the screen door and then his sister's clumpy steps on the stairs. Straining, he thought he also heard soft paws running up beside her and the tinkle of a bell.

"Now she's got me doing it!" he muttered.

The rain grew quiet, the wind died, waves gently washed the shore. The next time Filmore opened his eyes, it was nearly daylight. He pulled on his robe and went to his mother's room.

"What is it, Filmore?" she asked. Like Jodi, she always woke up at once.

"Let's see if Jodi really has a cat."

He took her hand as they went down the hall. "You don't believe there's a ghost cat, do you?"

His mother stopped in the hall. "Not literally, dear, of course. But Jodi does, so we must try to be understanding. She's still very little, you know. She isn't quite sure where reality stops and the stories of her mind begin."

"But why would she make up this crazy story?"

"We'll have to see if we can think of why."

Jodi's window opened on a huge dark sea and a rosy horizon. The sound of rolling waves was like the breathing of a giant in sleep. Jodi was curled under the quilt, her black hair shining on the pillow and Mrs. Tiggy-winkle under her chin.

"There's no cat!" Filmore whispered. "She made

the whole thing up!" He felt an odd mixture of indignation, relief and disappointment.

Jodi sat up brightly. "We're not asleep!"

"Did you and Mrs. Tiggy-winkle have a good night?" their mother asked.

"Yes, and so did the ghost cat. She stayed right here on my bed till she got warm and dry, and then she went away."

To Filmore she added, "If you don't believe me, look at this! She gave me her bell!"

Jodi opened her hand to show him a little rusty bell on a bit of frayed ribbon.

Filmore was going to accuse her of finding the bell on the beach, when he caught his mother's eye.

"Why did the ghost cat leave you?" their mother asked. "Doesn't she love you?"

"Yes, but she had to go because she was dead. Just like Daddy, you know."

Filmore saw his mother's eyes grow cloudy, but she hid them by hugging Jodi. He went and made a circle with them, turning his face away also.

Muffled by their arms, Jodi said, "That's why we're hugging and crying and smiling, right?"

THOR

 E'RE NOT

SUPPOSED TO HAVE DOGS IN OUR BUILDING, so we all thought it was strange the super didn't say anything when Mr. Prinz and Thor moved in. Nobody complained, though, because Thor was so well behaved. He never barked, he never smelled, he never made a mess. And he was beautiful, I got to admit that, glossy black like a Doberman, but muscular and huge, standing as high as his master's belt.

Right from the start I said there was something weird about that dog; but my friend Gabriel, he said I was crazy.

Gabe looks like a basketball pro. I mean he's tall as a post, with long wrists and great brown hands and a bush of kinky hair. And all old Gabe ever thought about was basketball, until he met Thor. After that it was like he was obsessed or something.

Nearly every morning on our way to school, Gabe and I would see Mr. Prinz and Thor out walking. Mr. Prinz was an old guy, straight and thin, with pink cheeks and tight, dry skin. He was a good walker, but sometimes Thor seemed impatient with the pace they took. But he always kept only one step ahead, and he padded along like a young soldier, strictly behaved. Thor never reacted to anything, not even to other dogs. What was even stranger, other dogs never reacted to him.

"So what?" Gabe said. "Who would dare mess with Thor?"

Thor was probably a male, with that name, but we never saw him either cock or squat. "So he does it private, so what?" Gabe said.

Once we stopped to say good morning to them, and Gabe offered the dog a sniff of his hand. It was the first time I ever saw a gleam of interest in Thor's eye, but Mr. Prinz warned Gabe off.

Gabe said, "So what? He doesn't want the dog to break discipline."

"Know what's wrong with you?" I said. "More heart than brains."

I thought Mr. Prinz was as strange as his dog. He didn't seem to have any friends or a regular job. He was always polite, even to us kids, but he never seemed to like anybody, not really. I told Gabe he was probably a refugee scientist or some foreign agent, with that accent of his, but Gabriel said he was just a lonely old man.

"Know what's wrong with you?" Gabe said. "More imagination than brains!" And he gave me this grin, getting even.

One day Gabe and I were starting out for school when Mr. Prinz got on the elevator by himself, carrying an overnight kit. He said good morning in his usual polite way, and Gabe asked him where his dog was.

"He cannot this time go with me," Mr. Prinz said. "I am going to hospital."

Gabriel, he always blurts out what he feels, he said, "Oh, Mr. Prinz, that's awful! Is it for an operation?"

"Not so, as I trust. I go only for the tests. I expect I shall be home by today or tomorrow."

"What about your dog? Can I feed him and walk him for you while you're gone?"

"No, he will be all right. You must not trouble yourself."

"It wouldn't be any trouble! I like him!"

"Never go near that dog! Never!" Mr. Prinz looked angry or frightened, I don't know which. As we were getting off the elevator, he became his usual stiff, polite self. "I thank you, my young friends, but

49

Thor is, how shall I say . . . ? An exceptional dog. You must please believe me, he will be all right."

When he was gone, I said, "Get that? Even Mr. Prinz says his dog is weird."

"He did not! He said special."

Gabriel watched every day for Mr. Prinz to come home. By Thursday when we still hadn't seen him, Gabe asked me to go with him after school to listen at Mr. Prinz's door.

"Here, Thor!" Gabriel called. "Here, boy!"

We couldn't hear a thing.

"Don't you think most dogs would bark or come to the door and whine or sniff or something?" Gabriel asked.

"Most dogs, but I'm telling you, Thor is weird."

"He is not! Something must be wrong."

"My dad told me to mind my own business," I said.

"Well, mine didn't, and somebody's got to call up Mr. Prinz."

We went to Gabe's apartment, and after three tries he found the right hospital. Finally a woman came on sharp and clear.

"This is Dr. Simmons, Mr. Prinz's doctor."

"I'd like to speak to him, please," Gabriel said, in his best deep voice. "It's important."

Dr. Simmons asked, "Are you a relative?"

"No, a neighbor. Mr. Prinz left his dog alone, and I think it's in trouble. I want to ask him what to do."

After a pause, the doctor said, "Are there relatives? Mr. Prinz listed no next of kin on his hospital forms."

Gabriel looked at me. I shrugged. "I never heard of any," he said.

"Did he have legal counsel?" the doctor asked.

"I don't know. Why?"

The doctor's answer was so low that I couldn't hear it, but I saw Gabriel's face go rubbery. "But he was only going in for tests!" Gabe protested. "He said he'd be home in a couple days!"

"It was entirely unexpected," the doctor said. "We had to operate. He didn't come out of it. I'm sorry. But now we must know what to do with his remains."

"His remains?" Gabriel was acting stupid.

"The body!" I whispered. "Tell her somebody will call back!"

He did and hung up, staring at me.

"Maybe your dad can do something," I said.

"What about Thor?"

"I guess that's up to the super."

None of us kids is crazy about the super. I mean, objectively speaking, Jenks is a suspicious old crud who thinks we all scratch graffiti in the elevators. He's lazy besides and won't do anything until it's serious, like you could wait forever if a faucet drips just a little, or only a few roaches run around the kitchen. Anyway, we went down and pushed his bell. He came to the door in his rumpled green work pants and ring of keys, with a fat sandwich in his hand. The sound of a ball game on TV came from his living room. He looked at us warily, chewing.

"It's about Mr. Prinz," Gabriel said. "He's dead."

Jenks stopped chewing and looked from Gabriel to me and back. Then he started chewing and talking at the same time. "If this is some kinda joke—"

"No joke, Mr. Jenks, believe me!" Gabriel said. "We just called the hospital. Mr. Prinz is dead, and Thor has been shut up in there four days! You got to open the apartment and see if he's all right."

"Listen, I can't—"

"You can and you better!" Gabriel said. "Or I'll get my dad to call the authorities!"

I don't know what Gabe meant by that, and maybe Gabe didn't, either, but anyway I'm sure old Jenks wouldn't like any authorities to see the condition of his building.

"All right, all right!" He put his sandwich inside somewhere and came back wiping his mouth.

We followed him to Mr. Prinz's. He unlocked the door and pushed it open slowly.

Gabriel called, "Here, Thor! Come here, boy!"

Nothing. In the hall was a coat rack with Mr. Prinz's beret and scarf on it, next to Thor's leash. We stood listening a minute, then moved on to the living room in a tight group.

There was Thor, sitting up in the middle of the rug, stiff as a statue in the park.

"Easy, boy," Gabriel said. "We're your friends. We've come to help you."

The dog didn't move, but I had this eerie feeling that he was watching.

"Look at that!" Jenks whispered. "He was told to stay, and that's what he's going to do till hell freezes over! I never seen nothing like it!"

Gabriel looked ready to cry. "Oh, good dog!" he said. "Good old boy!"

"Don't touch him!" the super warned. "Nobody make no sudden move. He might change his mind any minute."

We looked around, keeping one eye on the dog. There wasn't much to see, a couple shelves of books, a table with telephone and lamp, an arm chair, a radio and on the wall a year-old calendar with a winter scene of some European-type village in the mountains. In the bedroom was a cot made up tight as a drum, chest of drawers and an empty desk. The closet had two suits, some pants and a raincoat. The place was clean as a boat—no trash, no litter and only a smell of floor wax.

Gabriel looked in the bathroom and kitchen and came back furious. "There's no food or water for Thor! Not even an empty bowl!"

Gabriel brought water in a pan and set it down for the dog. "There you are, boy!"

Thor did not try to drink or even to sniff the pan. We might have thought he was dead on his feet, if he hadn't blinked and recoiled a little, as if he was afraid to get his fur wet.

"He must be in shock or something," Gabriel said. "I think he needs a doctor."

Jenks nodded. "Friends of the Animals Guild."

Gabriel didn't like that. "They put dogs to sleep if nobody wants them!"

"They have free vet service," Jenks said. "You got seventy-five bucks to pay a vet?"

We saw his point. Jenks picked up Mr. Prinz's phone and dialed. He did a good job of telling how urgent it was.

"Listen, we got a dog here, owner passed away. The dog is sick or something, and there's nobody to take care of him. No, this is the super."

He told them where to come, and we all went down to wait in front of the building. It wasn't long before a van pulled up and two dog catchers in white overalls got out. One was carrying a short stretcher, rolled up. He was hefty like a weight lifter, with a muscle-bound waddle and shoulders that looked like they would split his shirt. The other was young, maybe nineteen, with red hair and big eyeglasses. She had a rope and a net coiled over her arm and a paperback book in her hand.

"You the vet?" Gabriel asked both at once.

The big guy shook his head. "The vet couldn't come. We'll take the dog in. Where is it?" When he got a look at Gabriel's face, he added, "Don't worry, kid. Edie and me, we'll take good care of it."

"Did you bring your gloves, Joe?" Edie asked.

We all went back up to Mr. Prinz's apartment, but they wouldn't let us go in with them.

Soon they came out with Thor on the stretcher and no rope on him or anything. They carried him into the elevator with no more fuss than if he'd been a big toy animal. It was weird.

"I think he's catatonic," Edie said, pushing up her glasses.

They wouldn't let us on the elevator. Gabriel and I dashed down the stairs and Mr. Jenks came plodding after. By the time we got outside Thor was sitting up in the back of the van, staring out through the screen. Edie was in the driver's seat, reading her paperback, and Joe was at the curb with a clipboard, waiting for the super.

"What's wrong with the dog?" Gabriel asked.

"Beats me. The vet will have to figure that one. You can call up and ask him in two or three days."

"Two or three days!"

"It takes that long for the tests."

Jenks came out puffing and wiping his face. While he was answering Joe's question, Gabriel said goodbye to Thor. They were eye to eye, almost in a trance, until Joe got in the van and it started to pull away. Gabriel ran up and grabbed the door handle.

"Can't we go with you?"

"It's not allowed, kid. Sorry."

"But he needs me there when the vet sees him!"

"Come on the bus, if you want." He told Gabe how to get there.

Friends of the Animals was in a dingy building downtown near the river. It had a shop-front window with sixteen dirty little panes and a narrow door with peeling paint. On one side was an alley leading around back and on the other a vacant lot full of weeds and bricks. Inside was a dark green room, half office and half waiting room, with benches. From afar, beyond an inner door with a glass and wire window, came yapping and barking. There was a smell of dogs and disinfectant.

Gabriel opened the inner door, letting out a cold draft and a louder noise of yapping. "Joe?"

"Right!" After a minute, Joe stuck his head through the door and said, "Okay, fellas, you can come in."

We followed him through a large room full of empty cages to a white door with a porthole.

Inside, the smell of ether or something made me sick to my stomach. On a table under a moon-shaped lamp sat Thor, looking handsome and glossy black in that all-white surgery.

Gabriel went to him. "Hello, Thor! How you doing, boy?"

"Don't touch him!" I said. "Remember what Mr. Prinz said!"

A man in a lab coat came away from a sink, wiping his hands on a paper towel. He had a thick blond moustache but no hair.

"Hi," he said, smiling like a young guy. "I'm Dr. Bridgeman. This is not your dog, I understand? Belonged to your neighbor, passed away?"

I nodded.

"Why does he sit staring like this, Doc?" Gabriel asked. "He doesn't move or anything. What's wrong with him?"

"That's what we'll try to find out," the vet said.

"I don't think he's had any food or water for four days."

The vet dropped his smile. He wadded the paper towel and tossed it into the trash. "Well, I'll take a look at him."

He pulled a stethoscope out of his pocket and hung it around his neck as he moved toward the dog. "All right, fella," he said. "I'm not going to hurt you."

Thor sprang to a crouch. A warning rumbled out of his throat.

The vet froze.

Thor's lip rolled back from fangs like daggers in a huge red maw. His eyes fixed the vet with points of fire.

The vet slowly backed away. "All right, boy," he soothed. "I won't touch you."

The vet took Gabe's arm and pulled him slowly out with us.

Joe Kramer closed the door. He gasped. "That's a beast out of hell!"

We looked through the porthole and saw Thor sitting up as stiff as before. The lights in his eyes were just fading to deep points.

"That's a killer if I ever saw one!" Joe said.

"He is not!" Gabe protested. "He was frightened, that's all."

"Frightened like a panther!" Joe said.

"Is he a killer?" I asked the vet.

Joe and the vet looked at each other. "I don't know what he is," the vet said. "A guard dog, maybe. He doesn't want me to touch him, that's for sure. Something I did set him off."

"Maybe he's a war dog," I said, "trained to wait for the right command, no matter how long."

The vet shrugged. "We'll have a trainer look him over. Put him in a cage, Joe. He didn't mind when you handled him."

"You going to tranquilize him first?" Joe asked.

"Better not, in case he's already been drugged." He turned to us. "You boys might as well go home. We can't do any more today."

On the bus, I said to Gabriel, "Take my advice. Forget that dog."

"I can't! He needs me!"

"Yeah? If he's a war dog, he doesn't need anybody."

"What if he is a war dog! It's not his fault. Somebody did that to him!"

"More heart than brains!" I said.

Gabriel's father found out from the landlord

that Mr. Prinz had a lawyer, and he took care of everything at the hospital. There was a will but no relatives and no mention of Thor. So it turned out that Friends of the Animals would have charge of him. Gabriel's father said absolutely Gabe could not have that dog.

I was hoping Gabe would forget Thor, but Monday after school he asked me to go back to the shelter with him. We found Edie in the little office typing.

"Hello, you two," she said.

Gabe didn't even take time to say hi. "Is Thor eating yet? Is he drinking?"

Edie shook her head. "No, he just sits there, same as before. The trainer said he doesn't act like any dog he ever saw."

"What's going to happen to him, then?" I asked.

"That's up to the director."

"Could we see Thor, please?" Gabe asked.

"Sure." Edie led us past the surgery and down a long corridor. Rows of cages had dogs of all sizes and a few cats. The cats were all tucked in and silent, big eyes watching, but most of the dogs were barking. They would quiet to a whimper as we came near and stand at the cage door, tails just beginning to wag, full of hope. Gabe could hardly stand it.

At the end of the corridor in a big cage set apart

was Thor, nose to the wire. His water bowl was full and his litter had no stains.

Edie and I stood back and let Gabriel go up to the dog by himself.

"Hello, Thor! How are you, boy?" He offered a sniff of his big hand at the wire. They looked at each other eye to eye for so long I finally had to pull Gabe away.

Gabe began acting like he had a spell on him, or something. That dog was all he could think about. He forgot his homework and never knew what was going on in class. He even began to slip up in basketball practice.

That week Gabe phoned Friends of the Animals morning and night, but he never got Joe or the vet, and Edie always said there was no news. Finally Gabe told me we had to go back. We got there just as Joe Kramer was pulling out of the alley in the van.

Gabe shouted, "How is Thor?"

Joe stopped the van.

"Have you found a home for him?" Gabe asked, leaning in the window.

"Listen, fellas," Joe said, sort of pleading, "we can't place a dog like that, ready to go off any minute. Think of him with little kids, or somebody that couldn't handle him."

"What's going to happen to him?"

Joe pulled out a wad of handkerchief and scrubbed the back of his neck with it. "The director is right," he mumbled. "We can't watch the dog starve to death."

So they had decided to do away with him, I thought. I was glad! I knew it was the only way to save Gabriel.

Joe shifted into gear.

"Wait, wait!" Gabe cried. "You don't mean you've put him to sleep!"

"You want to hear the whole thing?" Joe said, almost angry. "You won't like it!" He turned off the ignition and climbed out. "The vet couldn't get near him to give him an injection, so we tried the tranquilizer gun. With a dose that would stop a lion. But he just shook off the dart and sat there, same as before. Then we tried the chamber. He stared out through the door and when the gas began to hiss he got this glow in his eyes, and that's all."

Gabe was staring at Joe stupidly. I said, "What do you mean?"

"He wouldn't die! I swear!" Joe's voice gave me chills. Gabriel's face was twisted out of shape.

"We kept checking the gas and it seemed okay," Joe said. "Finally the vet says, 'Turn it off, get him out.' He sat in his cage all yesterday. He wasn't even sick."

Gabriel started to smile. "Something was wrong with the chamber."

"The chamber and the tranquilizers both?" I asked.

"He wasn't meant to die!" Gabriel cried. "Don't you see! I'm supposed to have him! My dad will have to change his mind!"

Joe shook his head. "It's no use, I tell you. The director won't give that dog to anybody."

"I'll get my dad to talk to him! Don't do anything to Thor till then! Promise, please!"

Joe began to soften up. "Well, I'll see what the director says."

Gabriel took off for home like he'd heard a starter's pistol. Next day he looked happier, so I said, "Well, is your dad going to see the director?"

"Yes, but we got to make sure they don't do anything to Thor before he gets there. Come on!"

"We can't go now! We've got a math test this morning."

We went down at lunchtime, without even stopping to eat. Nobody was in the office, but Gabriel pushed through the inner door, ran past the surgery and on down the corridor. His great feet slapped the pavement like explosions and roused all the dogs to frantic barking. Even the cats sprang up. I caught up with him at Thor's cage. Gabe was looking around wildly. "Where is he?" The dog was gone.

Gabe saw another door at the end of the corridor and dashed up to it. Edie came out and barred the way.

"It's too late, Gabriel," she said.

Gabe shouted, "Joe promised—"

"The director would not change his mind."

Gabe danced from side to side and suddenly broke through her defense like in a basketball play and bounded through the door. We went after him.

Inside was a small bare room with brick walls and no windows. On the left was an open door to the alley, but the room was hot.

Joe stood there with his huge arms folded across a dusty black apron. In the burned wall behind him was a metal door, and beside it a bucket and shovel. Gabriel flew at Joe ready to punch him, but Edie and I grabbed his arms.

"Get the kid out of here!" Joe said.

Gabe broke away from us and braced himself against the door, breathing hard and glaring at Joe as though he was an executioner. That's how Joe looked, all right, guarding that evil metal door, but his face was more like a victim than a hangman.

"Please wait in the office," Joe said. "I'll talk to you later."

"Joe didn't want to do it, Gabriel, believe me," Edie said.

"Shut up!" Joe burst out.

"Don't tell her to shut up!" Gabriel cried. "I have to know what happened."

"You can't imagine how horrible—" Edie's voice was shaking. "How horrible to have to kill something that won't die!"

They all stood staring at each other with ghastly faces. I guess I looked the same.

Edie tried to take Gabe's hand, but he threw her off. "Joe did it with a karate chop. No pain, Gabriel, honest!"

Joe shouted, "Now will you go home!"

Gabriel started to moan. "I don't believe he's dead! Show me his ashes!"

"Go ahead, Joe," Edie said.

Joe turned back to the furnace. The handle creaked; the hinges squealed; the door clanked against the wall. A reddish glow of smoke poured out and a harsh smell like chemicals. Joe coughed and stepped aside.

"What's that?" Edie said.

"Beats me." When the air cleared, Joe pushed the shovel in and pulled it out. He set it down against the wall and beamed his flashlight inside. Edie went up to him.

"There's nothing," Joe whispered. His face was purple and sweating from the fire. He looked sick.

"You sure?" Edie said.

Gabe and I moved closer.

Joe pushed the shovel in again and scraped out a twisted bit of metal.

"Was that in there before?" Edie asked.

"I don't know. Anyway, there ought to be more than this. Bones, fangs! At least ashes!"

"He wasn't real!" Edie whispered.

"What was he then?" Joe asked. "What kind of thing just goes up in smoke?"

Gabriel burst out, "You're fooling me! You never put him in there. He escaped!"

He dashed out to the alley, shouting, "Thor, Thor!"

Edie told me to take Gabe home, but he wouldn't go home. We walked the streets until after dark, looking for that dog.

I tell old Gabe life isn't like school. In life you don't always get the answers. But Gabe says, "He's out there somewhere, waiting for me!"

All I can say is, if that's so, I hope they never find each other.

DAISY

NE DAY MY

MOTHER CAME HOME FROM COOLIDGE HIGH, where she's the librarian, and she stood in the doorway of my room, waiting for my attention.

The thing is, I was feeling low because we'd just lost our first game in the girls fourteen and under softball series and I was trying to read the life of Babe Didrikson, who never let anything get her down. I was in no mood to hear about carrying out the garbage or whatever I forgot this time. I mean, I know I have to help around the house, with just the two of us, but sometimes it's all too much.

Finally I had to look up. My mother still had her jacket on and her canvas bag on her arm and this smile instead of the frown I expected.

"Well, Abigail, you finally won out!" she said.

"Won out on what?" I could use the news of winning out on something or other.

"We have a dog!"

That brought me out of my chair. You got to understand how long I've been dreaming and talking about a big heroic canine companion, and all the while hearing from my mother, "No, no, we have no time for a pet."

"What is it?" I shrieked, dancing around her. "Great Dane? German Shepherd? Wolfhound? When do we get it?"

"We already have her! And here she is!" It was a regular fanfare the way she opened her bag and produced this little thing like a rabbit out of a hat. It sat on her hand, quivering and shaking and looking from me to mother with dark eyes bulging in its tiny round head.

"You call that a dog!" I yelped. "I call it a chipmunk!"

The little thing perked up its ears and tried to stand on trembly legs. Mother held it to her face. Its curly tail began to gyrate.

"Don't say that, Abigail! You'll hurt her feelings. She is very sensitive and very, very smart. She's a Chihuahua, aren't you, Daisy baby?"

The little thing gave a couple of yips and a yap and squirmed around to lick her chin. To be honest, I could see why mother would think it was cute, with its snub nose, big, brown, eager eyes and curl at the tip of its ridiculous tail. But cute was not what I longed for in a canine companion.

I flopped into my chair and clamped my hands over my face.

"I got to school early today," my mother said, ignoring my despair, "and there she was waiting for me outside the library door! Nobody knows where she came from, not the teachers, not the students, not the custodian!"

"Somebody is playing a trick on me!" I howled. I looked at the little thing. Her mouth was slit in a sort of grin, tongue hanging out, and she was huffing. If I didn't know better, I'd have said she was laughing, as though she had played the trick on me herself.

Mother sat down on my hassock, holding her cute little baby Chihuahua.

"How was the game?" she asked.

"We were destroyed! By the worst team in the league! Old Hoffmeyer said we were a disgrace to his bakery and if the Cupcakes can't do better he's going to feed us to the pigeons!"

"But I thought you had such a good team?"

"We have a great team! All but Hoffmeyer's niece. I mean she is the world's worst! She's got no fast ball! She's got no curve! Half the time she can't even put it over the plate! But she has to pitch or Hoffmeyer won't sponsor us!"

Mother waited for me to stop moaning before she said, "I thought you were the pitcher?"

"Not any more. Now I'm stuck on first base."

"But you're still practicing with Midge every day, aren't you?"

"Because Midge thinks some miracle is going to put me back on the mound."

I saw the Chihuahua watching my face, head cocked, gleam of interest in her eye, as though she understood every word. When she saw I was looking at her, she took a fit of delight and began to yip and yap.

"She likes you!" my mother said. "Want to hold her while I take my jacket off?"

"I'd sooner hold a chipmunk!"

The little thing stared at me with a mischievous glow in her eye, almost as though she was plotting something.

My mother is a tough librarian, I mean she doesn't take anything off those high school kids, but at bottom she's pure mush. That was obvious with Daisy, who could get anything she wanted from my mother, right from the first. Perversely, the little thing seemed to prefer me. She would look at me, head cocked, big ears alert, brown eyes sort of teasing, as though to say, "Like it or not, here I am."

"What do you want from me?" I would cry, as she danced around my feet, yipping and yapping.

I tried to put up with her. After all, she couldn't help being a Chihuahua and not the great noble dog I wanted. But when she would interrupt my homework or something, I'd end up yelling and throwing a wad of paper at her. She would dart away and run around yapping, pretending we were playing, but she really knew better; and when I would yell again, she'd tunnel under the rug.

Daisy was a puppy when we got her, but she grew up fast, at least as much as she was going to, and that was mainly in the ears. At first her ears were floppy, but they developed into great appendages that stuck out above her face like bows on a package.

There's this about my mother, she never takes a shallow view of things. Maybe that's the librarian in her. Anyway, after she got the little dog, she was always boring me with some new discovery from books.

"Toy dogs have been known for centuries. The Chinese loved them so much they used to carry them around in their sleeves."

"So send her to China!"

Another time she said, "Nobody knows for sure where Chihuahuas came from. One theory is their ancestors crossed the Bering Strait and bred with a Toltec animal called a Techichi."

My mother turned to Daisy. "Are you a little Toltec, Daisy darling?"

The little Toltec Daisy darling went spinning, "Yip-yip-yip! Arp-arp!" It was enough to give me a toothache.

"Anyway," my mother went on, "the Toltecs left carvings that look just like Chihuahuas."

"You should have brought home a carving!"

One day my mother came into my room and said, "I found out something else about Daisy's ancestors, but I shouldn't tell you. You'd enjoy it too much."

I shrugged and went back to my book.

"All right, since you insist," she said. "Listen to this. Dog fossils have never been found in Mexico, which means they probably had no dogs before Cortez."

"So?"

"So maybe that proves Chihuahuas did descend from Techichis. They say that Techichis were prairie dogs. Rodents. Related to chipmunks."

There's this great thing about my mother. She can take a joke on herself. She waited with a smile for me to scream with laughter and say, "I told you so!"

I said, "So?" and turned back to my book. She surprised me with a kiss on top of my head.

My mother did all this research, but I soon learned more about Daisy than she ever did, and not from a book.

Daisy didn't like to go out in the yard like any normal dog in our town. She wanted to be taken for walks on a leash, like a city dog. The first odd thing I noticed was that she would sit back staring at my mother and soon my mother would say, "Time for a walk, Daisy. Get your leash!"

I would say, "Mother, she just had a walk!"

"No, not today, dear."

My mother's memory of Daisy's earlier walk would be wiped out.

The next odd thing was Daisy's food. I would say, "Mother, you've already fed the dog!"

"No, dear, I must have forgotten. There's not a scrap in her bowl. Poor little darling, come and get your din-din!"

The poor little darling would have grown fat as a porker from extra din-din if she hadn't been running it off with extra walks.

I first understood the truth about Daisy on the

day of our next game in the series. I was late, looking for my mitt, and Daisy was chasing after me, tripping me, poking her nose into everything. I stopped and thought, "Try to remember! Where did you have it last?"

Daisy gave a yip, darted off and came back dragging my mitt like a fresh kill. She brought it to my feet and looked up, wagging triumphantly.

I was going to scold her for stealing it, when I remembered that she hated the thing. The first time she'd seen it, she had given it a sniff and backed away in disgust.

"Good girl, Daisy!" I said. "Where did you find it?"

She barked at me to follow her, just as a big noble dog would do, and led me to the dining room. Then I remembered that I'd left my mitt on the table with my books, and it must have fallen off behind.

"Are you psychic or what!" I said.

Daisy said, "Yip, yip!" and gave her version of a bow, head down, rear up, tail going like mad.

Sometimes I worried about what she was going to do to us, with all those powers of hers. But I had too much on my mind to think about it for long.

We lost our second game, and I'd just as soon forget it. Our catcher, Midge Elwood, refused to be discouraged, though, and almost every day she had me out practicing in the empty lot behind her house.

Midge is short, hefty and quick, just as a good catcher should be, and she has a voice that can be heard to the end of Bradbury Park. "You're the greatest, Abigail!" she would yell. "Nobody's got a fast ball like yours! Nobody's got your curve! Nobody is smarter than you and me together! Just hang in there, Abigail, baby! Our turn has got to come!"

We tried everything to get me back on the mound. We tried to reason with Orlene Hoffmeyer, but of course she would never admit that the trouble with our team was her. We even talked to her uncle. Midge said, "Listen, Mr. Hoffmeyer, if you want Orlene to pitch, the Cupcakes are going to lose. If you want us to win, you got to put Abigail back on the mound!"

"I don't got to do nothing!" he said, shoveling his cigar around in his mouth furiously. "It's you goils got to do something! You got to stop complaining and start working, that's what! My niece says you're a lazy bunch of fumble bees!"

So Orlene was still pitching when the Cupcakes came up against the Cooper's Dairy Buckaroos, the toughest team in the league.

Usually I ride my bike to Midge's and we go to Bradbury Park from there, but this time she came to my house. When the doorbell rang I grabbed my things and ran to the door, yelling at Daisy to keep away because I didn't want Midge to see her. I was embarrassed because the whole team knows how long I had been wanting a big, heroic canine companion. But of course Daisy beat me to the door.

I expected Midge to burst out laughing. Instead she fell on her knees, moaning, "Oh, isn't she beautiful!"

Daisy went head over heels with joy at this reception and dashed around Midge wagging and yapping. Then she settled on her haunches and looked at Midge, the way she does when she's concentrating her powers to some purpose.

"Let's take her with us!" Midge said.

"Are you crazy!"

"She'll bring us luck, Abigail!"

I looked at Daisy and saw her eyes grow bright and her tail give that eager little wag.

Midge bent over her. "What do you say, Daisy? Do you promise to bring us luck? Tell Abigail!"

Daisy jumped up and braced her paws against my ankle. "Yip-yip! Arp-arp!" Midge went hysterical laughing.

"And how are we supposed to get her to the park?" I said.

"She can ride in my basket."

"She's never been on a bicycle. What if she falls out? What if she jumps off and runs away! My mother would kill me!"

"Daisy won't run away!" Midge said. "She intends to stay with you forever."

"How do you know?"

"Don't ask me how I know, but I know!"

Daisy was an angel riding in Midge's bicycle basket, looking all around alert and perky on top of the big catcher's mitt.

Everybody at the park went crazy over her. We had a hard time getting the game started, with people crowding around: the players on both teams, all four or five of our fans and even Mrs. Tidcomb, the umpire.

Old Hoffmeyer went out of his skull when he saw the attention Daisy was getting. He shifted his cigar to the side of his mouth and said, "She'll be our mascot! With a little coat to match your shirts, Bo Peep Bakery! Beautiful! Such an advertisement!"

Daisy humped her back and drooped her tail. It was obvious to everybody but Hoffmeyer that she did not love him, with his loud mouth and smelly cigar.

"The little dollink!" Hoffmeyer stooped to pat her on the head with one fat finger and nearly knocked her out.

Finally Mrs. Tidcomb called, "Play ball!"

It was one of those blazing hot days when the grass is scorching and the sun boils your eyes, and it was going to be the hardest game of the series. If we lost today, we were out.

Lucky we were up first, because we can usually get a few runs to start us off hopeful. Daisy sat on the bench with our team, keeping her big eyes on the action.

First at the plate was Betty Blanche, our second baseman, a pretty reliable hitter and a fast runner. But the Buckaroos pitcher is one of the best in the league, a lanky, sinewy girl they don't call Flash for nothing. Right away she got two strikes on Betty, but then Betty hit a hard grounder that bounced off a rock in the infield and got lost between second and third. Betty tore down the baseline and crossed the bag just ahead of the shortstop's peg to first. We were hopping and screaming with joy.

Next up was our left fielder, Hilda Greenbaum, and she's a good hitter, too, but she was nervous and swung too soon and flied out to right field. Anyway, it was long enough for Betty to tag first and beat the throw to second.

Then our power hitter Frankie Washington came up, but to everybody's amazement, she struck out.

I had been swinging a few bats to loosen up, because I was next. Daisy leaned out to give me a sniff as I went to the batter's box. "Remember you promised to bring us luck, Daisy!" I whispered.

I took my stance and looked around to see where the fielders were and to make sure Betty Blanche was ready to take off.

Flash started her tricky wind-up and the next thing I knew Daisy had dived off the bench and was streaking across the infield. She flew at the pitcher's ankle, got a mouthful of sock and began yanking, pulling and growling with all her little might.

I threw down my bat and started for the mound as screams went up in every direction.

"Balk! Balk!" Orlene bellowed from the sidelines. "When you wind up, you got to pitch!"

"We get a base for a balk!" Hilda cried.

The Buckaroos catcher threw off her mask and let out a screech. "Are you crazy! That's interference! The batter is out!"

"There's no such rule!" Frankie shrieked.

Mrs. Tidcomb was saying, "Now be quiet, girls. It's my decision!"

All the while, our fans behind the backstop were whistling and laughing, Hoffmeyer was shaking his fist at the sky and yelling, "Play ball! You goils are here to play ball!" and Flash was dancing and howling, trying to shed Daisy.

Finally I pulled Daisy loose and carried her wild-eyed and quivering back to the bench. I scolded her about sportsmanship all the way.

By this time Orlene was ready to charge onto the field and slug somebody, but Frankie was holding her, and everybody on both teams was screaming and purple in the face. Mrs. Tidcomb had taken off her mask and was dabbing under her chin with her handkerchief, saying, "Please, girls! Decorum! Listen to your umpire! It's your umpire's decision!"

Then Midge stepped up and cried out in her huge, amazing voice, "Shut up, everybody! Our mascot made the pitcher balk! I say we owe Flash an apology!"

Midge is always fair-minded. "Midge is right!" I said. "Flash, we apologize!"

"But you don't get a base!" the Buckaroos pitcher yelled.

"And our batter is not out!" Orlene screamed. "There's no such rule about interference! Abigail, get back to the plate!"

Mrs. Tidcomb said, "That's my decision, girls. No base. Batter up! Play ball!"

Anyway, I popped out and Betty died on second.

As I guess I've mentioned, Orlene Hoffmeyer is the world's worst. The first Buckeroo that came to bat slammed out a double on Orlene's very first pitch.

Orlene walked the second batter and hit the third on the heel, so the bases were loaded.

Daisy saw me giving her pleading looks, but she had that face she gets when she's running away with my socks.

Flash was up next and hit a home run. So there we were, four to nothing and no outs in the first inning!

After that, the Buckaroos drove the ball left, right and center, all over the field. With every crack of the bat, Orlene turned and scowled at us scampering around after the ball, while runners kept strolling across home plate.

So it went like our previous games. The runs we got in our half of every inning were topped by the opposing team, because they smashed everything Orlene threw at them. Old Hoffmeyer must have been blind.

At the end of the fifth, the Buckaroos had us fourteen to eight. By now they were so overconfident they hardly tried, so we made two easy outs. The third one up took a mighty cut at the ball and knocked it to the sky over Orlene's head. Midge threw off her mask and got to the pitcher's mound while Orlene was still shading her eyes and searching the clouds. The ball dropped straight down to Midge for the third out.

You'd think that would bring us in running and cheering, but we were dead. Betty had bruised her knee on a long drive, Hilda had twisted her ankle and Frankie had sprained her thumb. We all had grimy, sweaty faces and squirrel-nest hair. Passing us on their way to the field, the Buckaroos looked smug. They still had us fourteen to eight.

We got no runs that inning and were headed back out to the field for the top of the sixth when I stopped beside Daisy pretending to fix my shoelace. "Listen, Daisy," I said. "Softball has only seven innings, did you forget that? You haven't got much time to keep your promise!"

Daisy turned her big dark eyes on me, and I knew she had something on her mind.

"I get it," I said. "You want me to apologize for scolding you, right? So I apologize. What could a Chihuahua know about sportsmanship in her very first game?"

She still looked expectant.

"What else can I say? You were a brave little doggie, trying to protect me!"

Still she was looking me in the eye.

"Little can be heroic! Is that what you want me to know?"

"Yip-yip-yip! Arp-arp!"

I rubbed her ears. She sat up and gave me a hasty lick. We had an agreement.

"Come on, Abigail!" Orlene shouted. "You're holding up the game!"

Daisy sent a growl toward Orlene on the pitcher's mound.

"Oh, no, Daisy!" I said. "You mustn't attack her! Think of another way."

As I started backing off to my place in the infield, I saw Daisy get that gleam in her eye. At first I couldn't see what she was staring at, then I heard a buzz and saw a bee hovering over Daisy's nose. For a moment Daisy and the bee were eye to eye and then the bee turned in midair and took off straight for the pitcher's mound.

"Not that, Daisy!" I yelled. Too late. Orlene screeched, threw off her glove, clutched her face and began stamping and howling. It was amazing how fast her cheek swelled up and shut her left eye.

Old Hoffmeyer ran out and led her off the field, calling for aspirin, ice, a blanket. Orlene leaned on him whimpering and hobbling as though mortally wounded.

"The game is over!" Hoffmeyer shouted.

"No, it's not!" Midge cried. "We got our relief pitcher right here!"

It took me only a couple of throws to warm up and I was on the mound at last. I could see the Buckaroos smirking. Naturally they thought our relief pitcher would be even worse than our regular.

Maybe I had some supernatural help from Daisy, I don't know, but the ball seemed to go out of sight before it reached the plate. The Buckaroos swung at everything, missing a mile, and the Cupcakes started showing some spirit in the infield, for a change.

"Way to go, Abigail!"

"You show 'em, baby!"

Our fans began to scream and whistle. Old Hoffmeyer stopped fanning Orlene and stared, so surprised that his cigar hung loose on his lip. I got three outs in nine throws and we went to bat knowing that nothing could stop us.

Daisy didn't overdo the luck. We beat them by only two runs.

Old Hoffmeyer said, "All right, you goils, you proved you can do better. So keep it up when Orlene gets back, or else!"

"Orlene's not coming back!" Midge said. "If Abigail doesn't pitch, Daisy doesn't mascot!"

That changed his mind, all right. Not even for Orlene would he give up Daisy and her little coat saying Bo Peep Bakery. And now there's no doubt who's going to win the series.

MICHAEL

"AUNT ROSEL?"

"YES, CARA?" AUNT ROSEL DID NOT TAKE HER eyes from her paperback mystery, either when she answered or when she dipped into the box of chocolate peppermints on the bench beside her.

"Don't you think there's something special about that squirrel?"

Aunt Rosel looked up for only a moment. "Where?"

"On the tree trunk there. His head is peering around at us." Cara adjusted her eyeglasses and pointed. "It's the same squirrel we saw yesterday."

But the squirrel was gone. Aunt Rosel offered Cara a peppermint, forgetting as usual that Cara did not like them because they burned her tongue.

Aunt Rosel went back to her book. Today it was Dorothy Sayers. Yesterday, Agatha Christie. Aunt Rosel read one a day, alternating her favorite authors. Sometimes she read the same book twice in a week.

Aunt Rosel had been with Cara and her father almost a month, now. When her father had told her that Aunt Rosel was coming, Cara had said, "Oh, Daddy, I'm so glad!" Mostly she was glad for him, because he needed someone to talk to in the evening. Manuela was good at cooking and cleaning but not talking, and anyway, as soon as she had cleared up after dinner, she hurried to the Bronx to cook for her husband.

As it turned out, Aunt Rosel was not good at talking, either.

Cara had pretended to be surprised that Aunt Rosel was coming, but she already knew. She had overheard her father's phone call to Nebraska.

"Rosel, I don't know what I'll do if you don't come! I can't face it alone. I watched her mother go this way, remember!"

Cara knew what that meant. She had known even before the doctors told her father. But it was all right. She looked forward to her journey, in a way. What she hoped most fervently was that the messenger would come for her while she was in her own room, or better yet, in Central Park. How wonderful it would be to set out for her long journey from a happy place!

Sometimes Cara wondered about the messenger, when he or she would come, how he would look, in what way they would travel together. It would not be her mother, Cara thought, but she was sure that her mother would be waiting when she got there, wherever it was they were going.

Aunt Rosel had arrived with a shopping bag full of paperbacks and little else. Cara got her promise at once that they would go to the park every day, if Cara felt well, and weather permitting. The weather was permitting most of the time, now that it was May, and Cara was clever at hiding how she felt. She would not try to smile, since a smile of pain was always suspicious, but she would make her face a blank, withdraw herself, and let the pain rage unattended.

Most of all, Cara wanted to keep her pain from Dr. Aspen, but she could not hide every sign of it, not the perspiration that would stand out on her forehead, not the trembling of her hands.

Sometimes the doctor would look at her accusingly. "You're very pale, all of a sudden." But pain is secret, and nobody can prove it, if you don't confess.

"You must tell me when it hurts," he would say. "That helps me to know how you're doing. There's no sense in trying to be brave."

Cara was not trying to be brave. She was not afraid of the pain. In any case, it always relented after a while, and peace would follow, peace that was sweeter than if there had been no pain at all.

"We have medication, to make it easy," the doctor would keep on. He was almost a nag about it. "There is no need for you to suffer."

Cara noticed with interest that he avoided her eyes when his own grew misty. She rather liked him and was sorry for him, in a way. But she would not take his medicine, even for his sake. It made her drowsy and sad. She would rather have the pain and sharp awareness. She wanted to be fully awake to every moment that was still her own. She would not let the doctor send her back to the hospital and confine her there and deprive her of each new day's adventure.

Now, in the park, she was pleased to see that the squirrel was back. "I think he knows us, Aunt Rosel!" she said.

The squirrel was coming down the tree head first, tail flowing after, little face held high. He was bigger than the others and rather fat, with a thick gray tail tipped in white and a white underbelly. He circled the bench and sat up before Cara, black eyes looking at her fervently.

"Don't call them, dear," Aunt Rosel said, flipping a page. "If you call them, they will never leave us alone."

Cara didn't have to call this one. Yesterday and now again today he had come of his own accord. He did not actually beg for food, but he leaped forward when she offered him a bit of peanut butter sandwich.

"Don't let it take that from your fingers," Aunt Rosel said. "They carry rabies, you know."

"Oh, Aunt Rosel!" Cara was offended. "Look how neat and dainty he is! Look at his beautiful teeth! He couldn't have rabies!"

"Rabies or not," Aunt Rosel said, "cut off his tail and what have you got? A rat."

The squirrel jumped back and scampered up the tree.

A moment later he was circling down again, followed by a small companion. They leaped to the ground and took turns chasing one another, chattering, "Cak-cak! Chick-chick-chick!"

Cara laughed. She was sure that the first squirrel had brought his friend to help amuse her, because often he would halt and look to make sure she was watching the fun.

"Cara-Cara-Carita!"

Cara sat up. Who was calling her?

"Cara-Cara-Cara!" Yes, it was the squirrel, and as plain as any human talk could be.

Cara glanced at her aunt, who was thoughtfully

pressing another peppermint between her lips. Aunt Rosel had not heard, and no use telling her. Aunt Rosel preferred to live in her mystery stories.

Cara listened for her name again. Disappointed, she decided that it must have been one of her brief illusions, convincing for the moment, but afterwards recognized as a visitation, like the pain, and part of the same process. She must not tell anybody, least of all Dr. Aspen. It would bring on his sighs and secret, thoughtful glances at her.

"We'll let you stay home as long as possible," he often said, "as long as you're comfortable, I promise." But she knew he was always trying to decide if it was time.

The doctor had a young face, thick soft eyelashes, a bald spot surrounded by short gold brown hair and a thin golden moustache. The effect was handsome.

Cara always noticed how people looked, even those she saw every day. Most people were handsome in her eyes, especially Manuela, who had strong brown arms and hands, slick black hair pulled tight by a rubber band, and dots of gold in her perfect brown ears. Aunt Rosel was handsome in a different way, pink and plump, with a delicate mouth, large, swimming, serene blue eyes and not a wrinkle anywhere, even though she was forty-seven, as Cara happened to know. Try as she would, Cara could not find any resemblance between Aunt Rosel and her father, although they were brother and sister.

Her father, however, was not handsome. He was gray around the lips and always frowning. His clothes hung loose and his posture was tired.

Cara was not handsome, either. She had a large forehead with blue veins and dark puffs under her eyes that her heavy glasses could not hide. Her arms were often bruised, from tests and injections, and so were her legs, from causes unknown. No one liked to look at her, especially the children in school, and for that reason Cara was glad she would not be going back. It was harder that her father and Aunt Rosel would not look at her, although she understood and did not blame them. It was because they could not stand to know what they knew. And that was the reason also for her father's frowns and Aunt Rosel's books.

Manuela looked at her more often than anybody else did, but that made her father angry. One night before Aunt Rosel had come, Cara had overheard them talking. Her father had jumped up from the dinner table, cup in hand, and followed Manuela to the kitchen, complaining that his coffee was cold.

Behind the closed door, however, he had said, "Manuela, if I hear you call her *pobrecita* one more time you will be in trouble with me!"

"Ai, si! Yes! Comprendo! La pobrecita!"

"What did I just tell you!"

"Si! Yes! Hokay!"

"She is not a pobrecita. She is gutsy! Gutsier than you and I, Manuela!"

"Gutsy, señor?"

"Valerosa! Briosa!"

"Ai, si! Gutsy!"

"All right! You understand! We are not to undermine her courage with our mush. No tears, no moaning and whining!"

Manuela gave one of her hearty sighs. "Si, señor. Comprendo. She is so valerosa, la pobrecita!"

Today, in the park, when it was time for Cara and Aunt Rosel to go, the squirrel was busy elsewhere. He had discovered an exciting spot in the ground and was working hard, forepaws throwing up soil, hind quarters quivering, tail in spasms. Suddenly he stopped, peered this way and that for Cara and came leaping after her and followed to the exit.

Waiting for the traffic light, Cara turned and saw him still on the walk, looking after her, tail like a plume, paws to chest, as though to say, "Don't forget me!"

"See you tomorrow!" Cara called. She waved, and he answered with a flourish of his tail and scampered away.

The next day, the squirrel was waiting for them as they turned into the park from Fifth Avenue. He ran ahead, little claws scraping the sidewalk, and often looked back to make sure they were coming.

"Those squirrels are everywhere," Aunt Rosel said. "They're like a plague." She did not realize it was always the same one.

Cara and her aunt settled on their bench and opened their lunch bags.

"Peanut butter again!" Aunt Rosel said. "We must ask Manuela for something else." But she began to eat her sandwich as absently as ever, turning her pages with amazing speed.

Hearing the rattle of her bag, the squirrel sat up with interest, but he did not beg. When Cara broke off a piece and held it out to him, he came forward, took it gently in his black claws and moved away to a courteous distance. He was a dainty eater, nibbling around the edges and pausing now and then to look at Cara with a nod, as though to say it was delicious.

"I think he's my friend, Aunt Rosel," Cara said.

"Of course," Aunt Rosel said, flipping over a page. "Who, dear?"

"The squirrel. He likes to be with me. I guess I couldn't have him for a pet, could I?"

For once, Aunt Rosel put her book down and looked Cara in the eyes. "Dear heart, of course you can't have it for a pet. It's a wild creature. You know what I told you about rabies, and it probably has fleas, besides!"

As though to confirm, or maybe to mock, what she said, the squirrel reached for his ear with a hind paw and scratched vigorously. Cara laughed.

Her laugh sent the squirrel into a frolic of chattering and leaping. His friend the gray squirrel was back, and they began chasing each other, squeaking and chirping, "Chit-chit-chit! Joke joke! We like you, we like you!"

Cara went stiff with listening. This time she was sure it was no illusion. "Oh, you *can* speak!" she whispered.

The gray squirrel ran up the tree. The bigger one turned to Cara, with paws to chest and an inquisitive cock of the head, as though inviting her to say something.

"What is your name?" Cara whispered.

The squirrel gave a flounce of his tail. "What you like!"

"Michael!"

"Kwa-kaw! Michael, Michael!" The squirrel circled and frolicked with delight.

"What did you say, dear heart?" Aunt Rosel asked.

"Nothing, Aunt Rosel."

"Wouldn't you like to go for a walk?"

Cara jumped up. It was unusual for Aunt Rosel to suggest moving off the bench. "Oh, yes! Let's go to the playground."

Cara waited eagerly, but Aunt Rosel made no effort to rise. Finally she said, "All right, dear, go along."

Coming from Nebraska, Aunt Rosel did not know that children should not walk alone in Central Park, not even at noon. But Cara did not tell her. There was nothing Cara feared.

Cara set off past the train of benches and the flagpole and walked through the trees, under the fresh, pale leaves and over the gently bobbing shadows. The park was full of people at noon, reading, strolling, eating bag lunches. Mothers and nurses moved slowly with toddlers or pushed strollers. People sat on the grass with sleeves rolled up, faces drinking the sunshine. A spaniel pulled his mistress on a tight leash, scurrying here and there to find smells.

Across the park was a roadway, with joggers,

skaters and bikers, and now and then a carriage decked with paper flowers, horse plodding, head low. The sound of clopping hoofs rang across the park.

Cara walked slowly, to take in every sight and sound. After a moment, she realized that the squirrels had come with her, frolicking sometimes ahead and sometimes behind. Michael would often look up at her, as though to share the pleasure.

The squirrels stood beside her as she looked through the playground fence. Everything was brilliant with color: swings, slides and benches in red, orange, yellow. A teacher had brought her class to the park and was waiting on a bench with the sweaters and lunch pails. The children filled the park with their shrieks and laughter, sliding, swinging, playing tag. Two girls, very good friends no doubt, sat on a tire swing together, giggling and swooping in wild circles.

The children were about Cara's age, seven or eight, but to her they seemed very young. Cara had not been a child like that, running, laughing and squealing, for years. She loved to see such happiness.

Aunt Rosel was still reading when Cara got back, and she went on reading even as they started for home and stood waiting for the traffic light.

"Wouldn't it be lovely to travel in the spring, Aunt Rosel?" Cara asked.

"Travel, dear?"

"I mean take your long journey. Just when everything is coming to life, fresh and new. Wouldn't that make a beautiful good-by party?"

Aunt Rosel looked at her suspiciously. "What do you mean, dear heart?"

"If you could choose, wouldn't travel in the spring be best?"

The light changed and Aunt Rosel took her hand. Cara could see that Aunt Rosel did not like the question and pretended not to understand, although perhaps she pressed her hand harder than usual. "Yes, of course. Traveling in the spring is always lovely. I went to Switzerland in the spring, years ago. I told you about that, didn't I?"

"No, Aunt Rosel. I'd love to hear it!"

But they were across now, and Aunt Rosel dropped her hand and was back in the mystery story.

The next day, Cara and her aunt had gone only a block toward the park when they were caught in a sudden rain. Aunt Rosel had her umbrella, of course, but she wanted to turn back. "You must not catch cold!" she said.

"But let's go to the entrance, at least!" Cara pleaded. "Michael will be waiting."

"Michael?"

"My friend. The squirrel."

"No, it won't, dear. Even squirrels have sense enough to go home when it rains."

"He'll be waiting! I know he will!" When her aunt saw her distress, she relented.

There he was on the sidewalk, standing as tall as he could, skinny and sleek in the rain, forepaws crossed, bright eyes searching anxiously. Faithful little Michael!

"He's shivering!" Cara ran to him.

"Come back under the umbrella!" Aunt Rosel called. "You mustn't get wet!"

As soon as he saw Cara, the squirrel's tail plumped up and was joyful. He leaped toward her.

Cara opened her lunch bag and tore off a piece of sandwich.

"Don't let him scratch you!" Aunt Rosel warned, as usual.

Cara knew that he would never hurt her, gentle Michael. He came close and looked into her eyes. His thanks were not merely for the food, but for remembering and coming.

He took the bread in his teeth and, with a farewell flourish, scampered off through the rain.

That night, the pain attacked Cara suddenly and unfairly in her sleep, when she was not prepared to defend herself. A cry escaped from her and woke her.

Her door burst open and her father and Aunt Rosel rushed to her side.

"What's the matter, dear?"

"I'll call the doctor!" her father said.

Cara sat up in alarm. "No, please, you mustn't! It was only a bad dream!" She was in terror of losing everything, the park, the party, Michael.

His father put his hand on her forehead.

"Any fever?" asked Aunt Rosel, straining forward.

"She does feel rather warm."

"But it's hot in here!" Cara protested. "Please don't call the doctor for nothing!"

Her father and her aunt exchanged a glance. "I guess she'll be all right until morning," her father said.

The next morning, Cara brushed her hair carefully and put on her prettiest dress. She did her best to eat a good breakfast. It was enough to fool them.

"Well, you must be feeling better!" her father said.

"Yes, I feel wonderful! I don't have to go to the hospital! Not today!"

Her father glanced at her aunt. "I'll see what the doctor says. Tomorrow is her regular visit, anyway."

Cara even managed to convince them that she was well enough to go to the park.

Aunt Rosel started on her book and her sandwich in the same moment, but Cara was not hungry today. Just their short walk to the park had made her tired, and her head felt strangely heavy. But today she was especially glad to have won her struggle to stay out of the hospital.

After the rain, the air seemed cool and tart as lemonade, and the grass and shrubbery were glistening. Sunlight was strung up in bright patches among the leaves, like lanterns for a party.

Michael was sitting up before her, paws to his chest. "Cara, Cara!"

As though to keep her from dropping off to sleep, he hopped closer. "Cara-Cara-Carita! It's time! Our journey!"

Cara sat up with a surge of new energy. "Michael, are you the messenger?"

"Come-come-come!"

She jumped up and was amazed to find how buoyant she was. "I'm so glad it's you!"

He stood tensely waiting. "I'm ready!" she assured him. "I don't have to say good-by. Nobody wants to know that I'm going."

She might have been wrong about that, because

dimly she heard Aunt Rosel trying to delay her. "Cara, oh, dear child! Not yet! Please!"

But there was no time left. Too bad that Aunt Rosel did not understand the joy. They would dance, they would romp, they would caper, she and Michael, all the way! It was happiness beyond any that she had imagined.

Michael went ahead, frisking and leaping, and Cara went after him, as agile and frolicsome as he; and that was how they went together, chattering with delight, along the path, through the trees, toward the misty, shining playground and beyond.

MANTIS

 WAS LATE

FOR SCHOOL, RUSHING AROUND LOOKING FOR the astronomy book due at the library, when I heard a tapping on the glass door of our balcony. At first I hardly noticed, because the wind does that with the ivy sometimes, but then I thought this tapping sounded deliberate.

Our balcony is dreary, with tubs of drooping ivy and dried-up evergreens, but it has a great view of sky over Riverside Park and would be marvelous for my telescope, except that all the stars and planets are drowned in the pinkish-poisonous glow of Manhattan.

Anyway, I found this praying mantis clinging to the ivy and tapping on the door with both forelegs. The little thing got so excited as I bent closer that I almost believed she had been trying to catch my attention.

I knew she was a female because only the females are bold and friendly. She was a beautiful, iridescent green, with huge mantis eyes the color of herself. But it was strange to find her there, because for one thing, mantises don't fly much, especially females, and we're on the fourteenth floor. Of course, I guess she could have blown up on the wind from Riverside Park.

But that wasn't all. This was April, and mantises don't hatch until May. They are born the size of mosquitos and live only one season. So how could this mantis be four inches long already and past her final molt, with full wings neatly folded down her back?

She looked normal, with four thin legs for walking and two great spiny arms that she held up in the typical mantis way, as though singing from a hymn book. She had a long thorax, a triangular head with delicate antennae between her eyes and the usual tiny fingers called palpi around her mouth. Like all mantises, she could turn her head to look back over her shoulder, just as a human does.

When I offered my hand, she put out her arms to examine it. She climbed on and turned up her little face in a curious and trusting way to look at me. It was funny and delightful.

"Well, where did you come from?" I asked.

My mother appeared in the doorway, fastening

her sleeves. "Lorette, you're going to be late! What have you been doing?"

"Looking for my library book."

"Astronomy again? I'll have to forbid you to borrow books if you let them interfere with your education. Have you combed your hair? Did you put on a clean blouse?"

She didn't wait for me to answer. "I've got an appointment with the hairdresser this morning and I want you on your way before I leave."

When she left the room, I turned to the mantis. "See why I wonder if it's worthwhile to take part in the human race?"

Grown-up behavior seems so silly when you consider the true ultimate reality, which is out in space.

I think about space a lot. Space has become so thrilling and fascinating and even dreadful to me that sometimes I can hardly bear it and wish I hadn't found out anything and could be simple again and brush my teeth and do my algebra instead of always seeing space in my mind's eye, with earth turning on a thread of gravity in a black, endless universe.

I found my library book in my locker at school, but the rest of the day was so rotten that I forgot about my mantis.

In the cafeteria, my friend Felicity went on and

on to Suzanne and Jeannie about these shoes she wanted. Clothes and looks mean more than anything to Felicity except maybe movies; and she hates it that the boys in our school have nice gray slacks and blue blazers while we have ugly jumpers. Finally she stopped long enough to stuff her face with chili beans, which for some reason made me think of something I wanted to tell them.

"Listen to this, everybody!" I said. "If the sun were a bag, how many balls the size of earth do you think it would hold?"

Felicity moaned. She tried to protest through her mouthful of beans, "Not your old universe again!"

Just then the new boy in our homeroom came along with his tray and stopped at our table. "Is this place taken?"

Jeannie shoved her books away. "No, you can sit there, Chesley."

Felicity groaned. Already she doesn't like Chesley, and only because his ears are like wings and his wrists hang out of his blazer. Anyway, Chesley sat there and began to eat his soup and crackers, keeping his chin well down to his bowl.

"So what do you think, everybody?" I said. "If the sun were a bag, how many balls the size of earth could it hold?"

Jeannie cried, "Oh, can I guess first?"

Nobody else claimed the privilege, so she said, "We know the sun looks little because it's so far away, but really it's big. So I will guess ten. The sun could hold ten earths."

"Guess again," I said. "What do you guess, Suzanne?"

"Who cares!" Suzanne said, with a glance at her leader, Felicity, to show her loyalty.

"I care!" Jeannie said. "So tell us, Lorette."

The new boy stopped but kept his eyes on his soup.

"One million!" I said.

Jeannie's gasp was highly satisfactory.

"But listen, Jeannie," I said, "the sun is only an average star. Did you know that?"

Her eyes were still wide. "I didn't know it was a star at all."

"It's true," Chesley said into his bowl. "The sun is only an average-sized star."

Felicity never likes it when she's not in charge of the conversation. She took it out on the new boy. "Mind your own business!"

His face went red and nearly splashed into his soup.

"The sun is everybody's business!" Jeannie protested. "Nobody owns the sun. Isn't that right, Lorette?"

"Right!" I said. "Chesley, you are welcome to the sun!"

Felicity sneered. "Aren't you going to thank her?"

The new boy managed to smile at me.

"Next question," I said. "How many suns do you suppose a giant star would hold?"

"You mean earths?" Jeannie asked. "How many earths would it hold?"

"No, I mean suns."

"Oh, wow!" Jeannie said. "Five? If it could hold five suns it would have to be awfully, awfully big!"

"Not five," I said. "Five hundred million!"

"Oh, oh!" Jeannie cried, holding her head. "Is that true?"

"Absolutely. I just read it in an astronomy book. That's intolerable to the mind, isn't it?"

"You're intolerable to the mind!" Felicity said, snatching up her books.

Suzanne jumped up with her. Jeannie asked, "Coming, Lorette?"

"Of course not!" Felicity said. "She has to run back to the library for some more science news."

In the library I found a book of telescopic photographs and took it to my algebra class. I hid it in my lap to look at pictures of Andromeda, a beautiful pinwheel galaxy with two hundred thousand million stars and my favorite because it's the same shape as our own. All at once I heard Sister Ursula say, "Lorette, you had better join us in reality."

I heard a snort from my former friend Felicity and then a whisper from Chesley, "She asked you to do question five!"

That was how it went, one thing and another all day long.

Back home after school, I was slumped on the living room sofa worn out with the stupidity of it all, when I noticed the tapping again, and there was my mantis.

"Have you been waiting for me all day?" I asked. "Didn't you even go look for food?"

I carried her to the kitchen and offered her a spoonful of water. She dipped in her little face to test it and then drank eagerly.

I speared a bit of hamburger on a toothpick and offered it to her. She picked it off, examined it, then jerked back and threw the meat away. She looked so shocked and disgusted that I decided she didn't like dead meat.

On the balcony I found a caterpillar and put it on her vine. She watched with interest as it humped along past, but she did not take it for food.

When I offered her a sliver of carrot, though, she ate it daintily, side to side, like corn on the cob, and cleaned her face and forelegs as a cat would do.

So I had found out another odd thing about my mantis. She was a vegetarian!

The next day at lunch Felicity led us to a corner of the cafeteria. "I don't want that cretin to find us again," she said.

"What cretin?" Jeannie asked.

"Chesley! I think he has a crush on me, the way he follows me around."

Suzanne giggled.

"I don't think he's a cretin," Jeannie said.

"I don't think he's following you," I said.

"Well, he's not following you, skinny shanks!"

I was waiting for a chance to tell them about my mantis, but Felicity asked if anybody had seen Burt Reynolds on TV last night, and she didn't say any more to me the whole lunch period.

As the others were getting up to leave, Jeannie asked, "Coming, Lorette?"

"Oh, let her sit there in her old universe," Felicity said. Then she decided to speak to me. "You're not the only one with science news! Listen to this. Cells take their permanent shape in your teens; so if you sit around and get a fat bottom now, you'll be stuck with it forever!"

That made me laugh. "A fat bottom is one thing I don't worry about."

She took that as an aspersion on her own anatomy. "I'll tell you some more science news! Why you haven't got your periods yet. Because you're unbalanced, that's why!"

I decided to tell Sister Ursula about my mantis, since she's my science teacher as well as my algebra teacher and my homeroom teacher. I went up after school and waited for her to finish stuffing papers into her briefcase.

Finally she asked, "Did you want to speak to me, Lorette?"

"Yes, please, Sister."

She sat down with a sigh, and for the first time I realized that she must be overworked. "Never mind, Sister, if you don't have time."

"Of course I have time! I want always to have time when my pupils need me. Otherwise, what good am I?" she said, with despair.

It occurred to me that her time might not be well spent on an insect. Desperate for something important to offer, I said, "I haven't got my periods yet, Sister."

With instant sympathy, she reached for my hand. "But my dear, you've just turned thirteen, haven't you?" Her eyes flicked over my jumper,

117

searching for the tardy buds of puberty. "Some girls don't start until they're fourteen or older."

"Thank you, Sister!" I turned to escape.

"Just a minute, Lorette. Are you worried about it, dear?"

"No, Sister. But the other girls—"

"Never mind the other girls. Each girl is different. Have you talked to your mother?"

"Oh, no! I mean, she—we—"

"I've noticed that you're not always attentive in class, my dear. You look a bit anemic, too. That could delay your development." She smiled. "Perhaps I'll suggest that your mother take you to a doctor!"

Stupid, stupid me! Snap off my tongue! I don't care if my development takes forever!

I went home to my mantis, who is so mysterious and intriguing she takes my mind off my earth troubles. She climbed on my hand, and her palpi and antennae began working in odd, precise combinations. She had done this before, with a curious concentration, but now it seemed to me that she was deliberately repeating the same moves. "I could almost think you were talking!" I said.

She stopped and watched my face. I said it again, exaggerating the words. When I stopped, she started, just as humans do in conversation. I put my ear to her mouth, but I couldn't hear anything. Either her sounds could not be registered by the human ear, or she talked in signs, like the deaf.

The next morning, I ran to my friends in the school yard where they were waiting for the bell. "Listen, everybody! I found this amazing—"

"What, another galaxy?" Felicity sneered.

Suzanne sneered, too. "Or some creature from space?"

I was stunned. For once, by accident, Suzanne might have said something intelligent.

After school, I approached the mantis with more caution. "What are you doing here?" I asked. "Are you friend or foe?"

I got no answers that I could understand, but I began to think about the earth from her point of view as invader from space. How beautiful and desirable it must seem! How precious in the universe must be our mountains and forests, our waterfalls, rivers and oceans, and all our amazing and beautiful life forms! I felt an explosion of love for our living green planet and a longing to save it from every harm.

At dinner that night I tried to think of some way to prepare my mother and dad for news of our invader.

"Do you remember what Shakespeare said? That there is more in heaven and earth than we dream of? Out in the universe, for instance—"

"Oh, not the universe again!" my mother exclaimed. "Lorette, pay some attention to what's happening here on earth! You've spilled gravy on your jumper! Go sponge yourself off."

She started on my father before I was even out of the room. "When will she ever grow up!"

"The boys will see to that, soon enough, with those eyes of hers."

By now the mantis was starting to worry me, although she hadn't tried to harm me, and for sure she gave me no insults. In any case, I thought I ought to see if we could communicate.

I started with parts of the body that we had in common, mouth, eye, foot. I would point to my part and then her part and say the word. She didn't seem to hear sounds, merely to feel vibrations, but she probably had other senses that I couldn't even imagine, and her eyes, with their many lenses, were much sharper than mine. Soon she caught on and began to make signs in return. I tried to imitate her language, but it was hopeless with my pitiful supply of appendages. She understood me far better than I understood her, I'm sure, but I began to recognize her meaning in a few little ways. For instance, every time I gave her food or water, she made a sprightly little move of her antennae up and down like a curtsy, which seemed to say not only, "thank you," but "you have made me happy." Whatever she was, spy, invader or courier, she was charming!

By Saturday, I was desperate to tell someone about her. After Mother left for the New School and Dad for his health club, I followed our cleaning lady around, shouting at her while she did the vacuuming. I broke the news cautiously, because Mrs. Henry has a natural aversion to bugs.

"Mrs. Henry, do you remember what Shakespeare said?"

"What he say, Sugar?"

"That there is more in heaven and earth than we dream of."

"Sure enough?"

"Take the heavens, for instance. There are wonderful, beautiful, terrifying things—"

I guess it was a mistake to say terrifying, although that's how I feel about space, sometimes. "Terrifying!" Mrs. Henry said, "ain't nothing terrifying bout heaven less you don't get there."

"But take black holes, for instance. Black holes—"

"What you talking bout, black holes?"

I got carried away, as usual. "They are giant

stars that have collapsed from the force of their own gravity, force so strong that even the space inside its atoms is squeezed out! Nothing can ever escape from a black hole, not even sound, not even light! So it's absolutely silent and invisible."

Mrs. Henry stopped the vacuum cleaner.

"Anything that gets too close is sucked in and becomes part of it and makes it even bigger and more powerful! And the theory is we have one, right in the middle of our galaxy, and that's where the power comes from, that makes all the stars go around."

"Listen here to me, child! That black hole sound to me like work of the devil! Better you get shed of that influence!"

In school, I began to see Chesley hanging around everywhere, after class, in the yard, at the library. He was always asking for the new science magazines that I wanted, then he would give them to me to read first. It was odd that when I started asking for nature and geology magazines, he did the same.

Just as I feared, Sister Ursula had a talk with mother, and I soon found myself on some doctor's narrow table, dressed like a paper bundle tied with string. While the doctor examined me, I tried to talk to her as one scientist to another, hoping to lead up to the subject of my mantis.

"No matter what you believe about the origins of life," I said, "whether it happened because of a certain combination of elements and conditions on earth, as some scientists say, or because God made us, as our cleaning lady and the Sisters say—"

"Breathe for me, please," said the doctor.

"Either way, it seems there must be life on other planets. I mean, the same conditions must occur on some of those millions of planets out in the universe. Or if God made earth, he made all those other planets, too, so he must have wanted life on them also, right? Otherwise it's duplication for nothing."

"You can get dressed now, child," the doctor said.

At lunch the next day Felicity and her satellites rushed to be first in the cafeteria and were settled in their corner before I came out of the line. I saw Chesley standing with his tray and soup bowl, looking around vaguely. Actually, I don't mind Chesley. He has sort of an appealing face, hopeful and honest. It makes me mad the way Felicity snubs him.

"Hi, Chesley!" I called. "You looking for a place to sit? I see a couple of seats by the window."

His face went red. He followed me, put his soup down, opened his crackers and didn't look up when he said, "I'm going to be an astronaut, someday."

"No kidding!" I said. "That's stupendous!"

His face got even redder and he talked about orbiters, landers and radar mappers until the period was nearly over.

All of a sudden, he said, "How come you're reading nature magazines now? Aren't you interested in space any more?"

Just then the bell rang, and Chesley hadn't even finished his soup. Anyway, it sure beat talking to Felicity.

Mother and Sister Ursula decided that if my problem wasn't physical, it must be mental; so they sent me to Ms. Dander, our school psychologist, who put me through her battery of tests.

Ms. Dander kept looking at my test scores as though she couldn't remember them. Meanwhile, I was looking at her, trying to decide if I should try to tell her about my mantis.

"Well, Lorette," she finally said, "you have done well. But I think you only half tried. Shall we do them again, to find out your very best?"

"No, thanks."

She frowned. "But it's important to know what one is capable of doing in life, don't you think?"

What I think is that if one decides to do anything in life, one will just do it, test scores or not. But I didn't say so, because she might take that as being against her reason for existing.

She said, "Isn't doing your best important? Is that why you settle for average when you could be at the top of your class?"

After a minute, she said, "Doesn't anything seem important to you?"

"Only the ultimate truth."

"Ah, but who can know that? I have a degree in psychology and not even I know that."

This rather amused me, so I said, "But I do. Want to hear it?"

She began to look at me with a certain eager suspicion and rummaged for a pad and pen, to take notes.

"Ready?" I said. "This is it. The sun is always losing hydrogen and gaining helium. In a few million years, if it follows the usual life of a star, the outer layers will start to expand while the core contracts and heats to about one hundred and forty million degrees centigrade. That's ten times hotter than it is now."

Ms. Dander's pen had stopped and she was looking at me blankly.

"That's hot enough to cause nuclear reactions in helium and form carbon," I went on. "Then come more and more reactions until the sun turns to iron. But iron doesn't give off energy by nuclear reaction. The sun will be dead."

I paused for the effect. "If that happens, the beautiful earth will be doomed. Now the ultimate truth is this. We must take care of our earth and keep it healthy for as long as we can and be ready when the time comes to move earth life to some new solar system."

I found Chesley hanging around in the hall outside Ms. Dander's room. "How did it go?" he asked.

"She wanted to know what I thought was important, so I told her the ultimate truth." I told Chesley the ultimate truth and he didn't have any trouble at all in agreeing with me.

I was surprised to learn that Ms. Dander reported I was normal. So she was smarter than I thought, and I was sorry I hadn't told her about my mantis.

My mother was annoyed with the report. "She called it a consuming interest," my mother complained at dinner, while my father bent over his roast beef, cutting and eating and hardly looking up. "I had a consuming interest, too, as a girl. My teacher said I could be another Emily Dickinson. But that didn't stop me from being sociable." Which just proves my mother understands Emily Dickinson about as well as she does me.

Anyway, I still hadn't found anybody to talk

to about my mantis; and I still didn't know why she was here, whether to do us earthlings good or evil.

That Friday, after school, I was heading for the bus when somebody called, "Hey, Lorette!" Chesley came running after me. Suddenly I knew that Chesley was the one to tell about my mantis. This time I offered few preliminaries.

"Chesley, do you believe in life on other planets?"

"Sure."

"Do you think intelligent life might evolve there in a different way? From insects, for instance?"

"Why not?"

The bus pulled up. As we were pushed along with the crowd, I whispered, "Do you think creatures from another planet might come to earth?"

"Sure."

People began shoving me onto the bus. I struggled to turn on the step and said, "I think I have one! Will you come and see her tomorrow afternoon?"

My parents were away the next day, but Mrs. Henry was still working in the bedrooms when he got there. I took him straight to the balcony. When he held out his hand, the mantis walked on and looked at him with as much interest as he looked at her.

"What makes you think she's from another planet?" he asked.

"She talks! Did you ever hear of an earth mantis that talks?"

All she did for Chesley, though, was explore with her antennae and make ordinary insect motions.

We took her to the kitchen, where Chesley put her on the table and gave her a slice of apple. She made her little curtsy.

"That means thank you!" I said.

Chesley gave her a spoonful of water, and when she thanked him again, I could see that he was starting to believe it.

"Listen, Chesley," I said. "She is beautiful and charming, but what if she's a spy? Preparing for an invasion?"

I told him that thinking of earth from her point of view made me realize the ultimate truth: how precious the earth is and what we must do. Chesley listens well. It's one of his best qualities.

"I'm sure she has a message for us, a threat or a warning, I don't know which. But whatever it is, we have to translate it! Will you help me?"

"Sure!"

Just then I heard Mrs. Henry. "Lorette? Who you talking to, Sugar?"

"It's the cleaning lady!" I said to Chesley. "Hide the mantis! She hates bugs!"

"This is my friend Chesley from school," I said. "Chesley, this is Mrs. Henry."

Mrs. Henry broke into a grin. "So you brought home a boyfriend stead of all them books for a change! Your mama will be happy for that!"

Chesley said, "How do you do, Mrs. Henry?" but he was squirming with his hands behind his back, trying to lure the mantis to crawl on, and I must say he looked peculiar.

Mrs. Henry's smile turned doubtful. "Well, we got to start someplace."

I tried to create a diversion. "Mrs. Henry, could we have some brownies and milk?"

"Sure enough, Sugar. You and your boyfriend sit right down."

As she moved toward the refrigerator, she caught sight of the thing on the table. "Oh, oh! What's that?"

She shoved Chesley aside, grabbed a handy roll of paper towels and lunged at the mantis.

The mantis hunched in shock and looked up at me, bewildered.

"Wait!" I shrieked, as Mrs. Henry raised her arm to strike.

The mantis stood up and unfolded two pairs of rose-colored wings, shimmering and beautiful as an evening dress. Mrs. Henry froze, mouth open, weapon in hand. The mantis fanned the air, lifted off the table, fluttered to the ceiling and out the kitchen door.

Chesley and I ran after her as she made for the balcony.

"Please don't go!" I called.

The mantis flew out and away on an updraft of wind. I leaned over the rail and watched her dipping and rising, fluttering, glinting and soaring, growing smaller and smaller until she disappeared into the haze over Riverside Park.

"Better it be outside, anyhow, Sugar," Mrs. Henry soothed. "Can't no butterfly live indoors."

I realized that I was crying.

Chesley managed to eat quite a few brownies, but I had no appetite. "She was no danger to us," I said. "We were a danger to her! And we made her fail her mission. I never got her message."

"Maybe you did, you know," Chesley said, licking chocolate off his fingers. "Maybe her message was the ultimate truth."

Until then I guess I had always sort of pitied Chesley, and when you pity somebody you look down on him. I would never look down on Chesley again.

RONDO

ASKELL AWOKE

THINKING HE WAS IN BED AT SCHOOL, LATE again for Latin with old Gosbeck, who hated his guts. He did not hurry to get up. Things were already so bad that being late again wouldn't make much difference.

Then he saw the rocking chair and his suitcase and remembered that he was at his grandparents' house, in the room that had belonged to his mother. He felt no better.

The porcelain clock on his mother's dressing table said it was almost noon. He got up only because he was hungry.

"Ah, there you are, my boy!" his grandfather said, as he went into the kitchen.

Maybelle, who had been with his grandparents for as long as Haskell could remember, was putting a vase of rosebuds on a tray. "You sure one sleepyhead this morning, ain't you, Haskell!" Maybelle said,

133

laughing. It occurred to Haskell that Maybelle was too familiar for a servant.

His grandfather was not the great burly giant that Haskell remembered, but a rosy cheeked old guy with a white moustache and dentures that clacked. "Shall we take this tray to your grandmother and say hello? She has been asking for you."

Haskell would rather have had lunch first, but he followed his grandfather to the bedroom at the end of the house. His grandmother looked as withered and tiny as an old doll propped up in the huge bed. She smiled and held her blue-veined hands out to him shakily.

"Dear Haskell! We are so glad to have you back! Do you know how long it's been? My goodness, look at the size of you! Come and kiss me!"

Her hands were cold. Her kiss on his cheek was as soft as a powder puff.

"I'm getting up today in your honor!" she said. "I'm going to have dinner with you and Granddad in the dining room!"

"Esther, dear—" his grandfather began.

"Now don't you say I mustn't, Jesse. It will do me wonders of good!"

At lunch, Haskell grew irritated by the old guy's teeth, which clicked as he chewed. When it became unbearable, Haskell pushed away from the table and went out without a word.

He remembered that there had once been a pony and a cow in the barn. Now he found the stalls empty, hot and dry, with cobwebs in the corners and dust floating in rays of sunlight.

He went out and sat on a sawhorse dejectedly. How was he going to stand it here? It was even more boring than school.

A horse whinnied in the distance. Following the sound, Haskell crossed the field, climbed a rise and broke through a growth of shrubberies, tearing off a switch to carry with him. He came out looking down on a ring where a girl in chaps was taking a bay horse through a course of jumps. She looked a few years older than Haskell, about sixteen. Her dark shining hair bounced as she rode. She was concentrating hard, and so was her horse. Haskell went down to the ring.

The horse sensed his presence and broke stride. Haskell went up and hung over the fence.

"Give him more leg!" he called, grinning. "Kick him, then he won't slow down on you like that."

The horse and girl approached slowly. "Where did you come from?" she asked.

Haskell waved toward the gap he had made in

the shrubbery. "My grandparents. I'm staying there till Granddad finds me a decent school."

The girl warmed. "Then you're Haskell! Your grandparents have been looking forward so much to your visit, Haskell!"

"At school they call me Hassel." He grinned.

She did not take note of that. "I'm Wendy Bethune." She thumped her horse on the neck. "And this is Rondo. Rondo, this is Haskell, our neighbors' grandson."

Haskell snorted. "You talk to your horse?"

"Always. He understands everything."

"Ha, ha! He doesn't look so smart to me. He's just an old grade horse, isn't he?"

"No, Rondo is a Thoroughbred. And he's not old. He's not even four, yet."

Haskell did not like her patience. He began to switch the fence. He was gratified to see the bay start shuffling.

"Please don't do that," Wendy said. "Rondo thinks you're threatening us."

Haskell laughed. "I told you he was stupid!" He slashed the fence again.

"Drop that stick!"

Haskell dropped it, but angry with himself for obeying the order, he picked it up again.

"You'll have to excuse us, please," Wendy said. "We're trying to get ready for a show."

"Okay, you're excused," Haskell said, but he stayed on the fence.

"I mean go away! You're making Rondo nervous." Wendy turned her horse back to the ring.

"It's not your horse, it's you!" Haskell shouted after her. "Get off and let me show you how to handle him!"

Wendy turned the horse again. He picked up and came straight toward Haskell, ears back, eyes white with anger.

"Get off the fence, Haskell!" Wendy ordered.

Haskell jumped down. "I'm not afraid of your stupid plug!"

Moving away, he yelled, "You stink!"

Haskell idled around the field, staying away from his grandparents' house as long as possible. When it grew chilly, he went back in through the kitchen.

Maybelle looked up from the oven with a shake of the head. "Where you been keeping yourself?" she asked. "They been waiting and waiting for you."

His grandparents were already in the dining room. His grandmother, dressed in an embroidered robe, was in a wheelchair, with his grandfather beside her, in a tie and jacket. The table was set with crystal and silver and a great bowl of salmon-colored roses.

His grandparents talked to him cheerfully and did not mention his troubles at school, but Haskell concentrated on the ham and fresh beans and seldom looked up. He had forgotten that Maybelle was a good cook.

Finally, after Maybelle brought in pecan pie, his grandfather asked, "Where did you go this afternoon, Haskell?"

"Just around."

"You were gone for hours, dear," his grandmother said. "You had us a little worried."

"What am I, a baby?"

They looked surprised. "Of course not," his grandmother said. "We wanted to talk to you. It's been a long time since we've seen you."

"And we promised your parents we wouldn't let you out of our sight!" His grandfather laughed. "They're a long way off, you know!"

"I went to the neighbors," Haskell finally answered.

His grandmother brightened. "To Bethunes'? Did you meet Wendy?"

"Who are those people, anyway?" Haskell demanded.

"They bought the old Langston place, don't you remember?"

"He wouldn't remember that, Esther," his grandfather said. "That was after he went away to school."

"Yes, but we wrote him about it. Didn't we, Haskell?"

"I don't remember."

"Well, there is George Bethune, the father, and Patricia, the mother, and their two daughters, Josephine—she will be starting to state university in the fall—and Wendy—she's still in high school."

His grandfather was smiling as though that was the most interesting thing he had ever heard. "Wendy is a very accomplished young lady," he added. "She has a champion horse, Rondo, that she raised herself, from the day he was born."

"He didn't look so great to me."

"Oh, yes! Wendy has a shelf full of trophies in her tack room. Ask her to show them to you."

"Who cares!" Haskell said.

His grandparents looked at him with dismay.

"I've seen a million boring tack rooms and a million boring trophies. We have riding at school, you know. I've won trophies myself." This was not a lie, Haskell felt, since he had won ribbons, although never a blue one. Haskell had been barred from riding this term because the instructor said he was cruel to the horses. That was unfair. The hacks were stupid. He would be able to ride as well as anybody, if he had a horse of his own at school, like some boys.

Haskell did not believe that Rondo's trophies could amount to much. He decided to see them for himself. The next morning, early, he crossed the field and pushed through the shrubbery.

The Bethune house was set back among great trees, at a distance from the stable and paddock. He approached the stable cautiously, until he was sure no one was about. Rondo was alone, munching hay from a rack in a corner of the fence. Haskell paused in the stable door. The smell of the stable roused the old fear and defiance that he had always felt in riding class and, in fact, in every class at school.

Wendy came in through the back, trundling a wheelbarrow. Startled, and to cover his guilty intrusion, he shouted at her, "Hey, Wendy! When are you going to let me ride your stupid old hack?"

"Good morning, Haskell," she said cheerfully.

"Well?" he demanded.

"If you mean Rondo, the answer is never."

She trundled the barrow to a stall. Haskell sauntered in to watch her fork manure into the barrow. "You afraid I'll show you up?"

"It's not just you, Haskell. Nobody rides Rondo but me. I'm schooling him. I told you that."

"I'm not just anybody!" he protested. "I've had riding at school, you know. From the very best masters. I can probably ride better than you!"

A nicker came from the far stall.

"You got another horse?" Haskell asked.

"That's Duchess, Rondo's dam. She's asking what the fuss is about."

"I guess you're going to tell me I have to ride the old dame!"

"Dam, Haskell, not dame."

"I know that! Can't you take a joke!"

She cast a sour look at him as she shoveled another forkful into the barrow. "Stand aside, please."

"Well? Are you going to tell me I have to ride the old dame?"

"No, you can't ride Duchess, either. She's lame. If you want to ride, there's a stable not far from here. They have good horses. And there's a pretty trail up through the woods. Maybe your grandfather will take you."

"I don't need anybody to take me! I've ridden all kinds of trails! And better horses than Rondo!"

Wendy leaned on her fork and looked at him thoughtfully. "Why do you act this way, Haskell?"

It was a question he had heard before and did not like. "The hell with you!"

"You'll have to excuse me now."

"Why don't you say get lost when you mean get lost!"

"I would, if I didn't like your grandparents so much!"

Haskell laughed, delighted to get a rise out of her at last.

"Stay away from Rondo!" she called after him. "You could get hurt."

"I'm not afraid of your stupid old horse!"

Strolling out, Haskell passed a bush at the stable door and broke off a switch. He held it behind his back as he ambled toward the paddock. Rondo cast an eye at him, but went on munching hay.

Haskell hung over the fence. "He's not so much," he told himself. "I could handle him easy. Bareback, just as he is."

He began to idle along toward the horse. It would be no trouble at all to mount him now, lined up as he was along the fence. Anyone could climb the rail, drop to Rondo's back, grab his mane, whack his rump to distract him from the hay and take him for a canter around the paddock. Wendy would come out and see that she was not the only one who could ride her horse. Dumb girl.

Of course he didn't intend to do it. As he drew near, however, Rondo flicked an ear at him, nickered and shifted away from the rail. Haskell saw that the horse might leave the fence at any moment, and his chance would be gone.

He climbed to the top rail, stepped over, dropped onto Rondo's back and snatched his mane. Rondo caved in under him a moment, looked in surprise over his shoulder.

"Go, go, you stupid plug!" Haskell shouted, and gave the horse a great slash on the rump.

With a neigh of anger and fear, the horse leaped out into a terrible run, faster than Haskell could have imagined. He fell to the horse's neck and clung with his legs. Shouting, "Whoa, whoa!" he thrashed the horse wherever he could reach.

In a frenzy, Rondo began to rear, wheel and buck. Haskell brought the switch down harder. With a scream of pain, the horse dashed back toward the stable. Wendy was running out with a halter.

"Hang on, Haskell!" she shouted.

As she came through the gate, she saw Haskell raise his arm. "Drop that switch! You're making him crazy!"

The horse threw himself against the fence and tried to scrape Haskell off. The rail splintered, ripped Haskell's jeans and pulled at his right leg.

Trees, fence and stable went spinning against the sky. The ground rose up, slammed into him and pushed the breath out of him. He heard a shriek from the horse. In dread of being trampled, he rolled over and staggered to his feet. He saw that the horse was down, churning the dust.

Wendy dashed toward Haskell, but he got away from her and scrambled through the gate.

"You haven't taught that horse one damn thing!" he shouted, backing off.

Wendy turned from Haskell and ran to the horse. Rondo grew quiet as she approached, rumbled in his throat and bobbed his head at her. Afraid that something terrible had happened, Haskell looked back from a safe distance. The horse struggled to rise at Wendy's urging and finally got up on three legs. His right foreleg was dangling useless and pumping blood.

Wendy sobbed, "Oh, Rondo!" She tore a strip off her shirt, tied it above the wound, shouting at Haskell, "Call my mother! Tell her to get the vet! Hurry!"

When she saw Haskell backing away, she dashed out of the paddock and ran to the house, calling, "Mother! Mother!"

Haskell limped home and stole into the bathroom to wash his cut. He changed his torn jeans and fell onto his bed.

He was still there when his grandfather looked in to say that it was time for lunch.

"I'm not hungry, Granddad."

"Feeling all right?"

"I have a headache. I want to take a nap."

At dinner time, Haskell combed his hair and put on a tie and went to join his grandparents in the dining room. It had occurred to him that he might need allies. He gave them a broad grin.

"Feeling better, Haskell?" his grandmother asked.

He did his best to be charming, told them funny stories about school and said how much he liked Maybelle's meat loaf.

"Grandmother, is this the ketchup we made?"

"Don't tell me you remember that, Haskell! That must have been six years ago. You were only a little boy!"

"Of course I remember! We worked in the garden, you and I, and grew so many tomatoes we didn't know what to do!"

Haskell warmed to his grandparents' laughter. He recalled that he had enjoyed chopping the soil with his own red-handled hoe. The hot earth had smelled good enough to eat, and the sun had warmed his back. He remembered the look of his grandmother, then plump and rosy, in her denim apron and the broken straw hat that cast sequins of light on her chin.

"We finished that ketchup long ago," she was saying.

"The pickles and apricots, too?"

His grandmother beamed. "I haven't done any canning for a long time."

"Grandmother, you canned the best everything I ever tasted!"

His grandparents were glowing by now. People were so easy, Haskell thought. It was as easy to make them happy as it was to make them mad.

The telephone rang. Maybelle put her head through the kitchen door. "Y'all want me to take a message, Mr. Clayton?"

"Yes, please, Maybelle."

Haskell hunched over his plate. At last Maybelle returned and Haskell felt her eyes on the back of his head.

His grandmother asked, "Who was it, Maybelle?"

"Josephine."

"Is something wrong?" his grandfather asked.

"Yes, sir, something wrong. Mighty wrong!"

"Maybelle, what is it?" His grandmother faltered. His grandfather took her hand.

"Josephine say don't take y'all from dinner, but it's Rondo. They had to put him down."

A gasp of horror went up from his grandparents. They asked, together, "What happened?"

"He broke his leg this morning. The vet say no hope. Put him out his agony."

Haskell fought an impulse to dash from the table.

His grandmother had begun to cry. His grandfather got up and put an arm around her. "How?"

"He fell."

"With Wendy?"

"No, in the paddock. I can't say no more than that, Mr. Clayton, sir." After a pause, she added, "Josephine say they want to know how is Haskell?"

"How is Haskell?" his grandfather repeated.

"I told her Haskell look all right to me. I don't see no broken leg on Haskell."

His grandparents looked at him.

"I scratched my leg, that's all," Haskell muttered.

His grandfather kissed his grandmother. "I must go right over, Esther."

"Yes, of course, Jesse! Find out if there's anything we can do. Tell Wendy how sorry we are." She turned to Haskell. "We loved Rondo, too, you know."

"Want to come along, Haskell?"

"No, thanks, Granddad. I'll stay with Grandmother."

"Thank you, dear." His grandmother smiled. Shame stirred in Haskell that he was staying to avoid the Bethunes and not to comfort his grandmother, as she thought.

Maybelle wheeled his grandmother to her room. Haskell followed and did what he could to help get her settled. He sat on the bed and talked with his grandmother about the memories they shared.

"You were a delightful child," his grandmother said. "So imaginative. So witty, keen and sensitive. So helpful and loving. Your grandfather always said you had a brilliant future."

What was the matter with his grandparents, Haskell wondered. Didn't they realize the truth about him? That he never did anything right? That he made trouble wherever he went? That everybody hated him, and he hated everybody? But his grandmother was smiling and utterly sincere. It occurred to Haskell that what she said might have been true, once. He had been happy, long ago, and had liked himself better, and yes, he had loved his grandparents. Suddenly he did not want them to change their opinion of him.

Now he felt even more anxious about his grandfather's return. At last he heard a slow step in the hall. His grandfather came in and stood at the foot of the bed.

"Rondo fell, somehow, against the fence," he said.

"Just fell?" his grandmother asked.

"So it seems." His grandparents were glued to each other's eyes. Their tears were brimming. "Wendy and I had a long talk. She will be all right. She's a remarkable girl."

Haskell felt sure that his grandfather was not going to worry his grandmother, even if he knew the truth. He felt safe enough to leave them and go to his room.

But he could not sleep. It seemed that he heard the neighing of a horse for hours as he thrashed under the covers, hot and cold by turns.

He threw off the covers and went out to the living room. His grandfather was alone there, with a book turned over on his lap, his eyes closed. He roused himself.

"What's the matter, my boy? Can't you sleep?"

"I keep hearing that horse."

"That's Duchess, calling Rondo."

Haskell shifted from foot to foot. "You mean she misses him that much?"

"Yes. She's worried about him. She knows he should be in his stall by now."

Haskell snorted. "Some horses care more about their sons than people do."

His grandfather looked at him thoughtfully. "I wonder if that's what you think about your own parents?"

Haskell turned away.

"You know, you were too young at the time to be told why your parents went abroad without you."

"What do I care!" Haskell felt his throat constrict. "I didn't want to go with them, anyway!"

"Your father was assigned to a hardship post. They didn't want you to know."

Haskell brushed his face with his pajama sleeve. "What's a hardship post?"

"A country where there is political unrest or difficult living conditions."

"You mean dangerous?"

"Yes. But later when your parents got a new assignment, you refused to leave school."

"I was having too much fun!" Haskell said, bitterly.

"We wanted you to come and live with us as

soon as your grandmother got out of the hospital. But you wouldn't do that, either."

Haskell could not speak. He was not sure he knew why he felt as he did, and he was struggling to hold off tears.

"If you ever change your mind, you would make your grandmother and me very happy."

Haskell walked about restlessly behind his grandfather's chair. The room was filled with the sound of anxious neighing.

"Why doesn't somebody stay with that horse?" Haskell said, gruffly.

"Wendy has been with her most of the day. But Duchess wants Rondo. It will be a long time before she forgets."

Haskell sneered. "I don't believe horses are that smart!"

His grandfather smiled. "You used to think Doughboy was smart enough to be in the circus. Remember Doughboy?"

"Yes, where is he?"

"Doughboy was old even when you knew him. We wrote you when he died, don't you remember?"

That must have been one of their many letters that Haskell had not bothered to read. He began pacing again.

"Let's go have some warm milk," his grandfather said. "It will help us sleep."

It was late when Haskell went back to bed. Just as he fell asleep, he was sure he heard two horses neighing, one calling and the other answering.

He awoke with a start to a black, smothering silence. For a moment he thought he must be in a coffin. Some hideous noise had passed over and was gone, leaving a vibration in the air. Haskell's cold, tingling arms would not respond. His heart was lashing in his chest.

He felt hot, rumpled sheets and knew that he was in bed. Was it a nightmare that had waked him? He could not remember. Now he could see a faint rim of light circling the window. He could sense a rumbling, a certain tremor in the ground. The rumbling grew heavier and he realized that it was a pounding, perhaps galloping.

Compelled to see what it was, he pulled himself up on trembling legs and went to the window. On the lawn, a great horse was running in a circle, as though on a lone line. Moonlight glistened on his sweating back. His ears were flat to his skull and his eyes flashed. He turned this way and that, trying to be free of the line, but there was no line and no trainer. Now the vibration from his hoofs was thunderous, and Haskell saw that his right foreleg was gory.

The horse pulled up, fixed on Haskell, broke free and charged. He loomed enormous at the window, lips stretched wide around great, square teeth. He reared and his hoofs went high over Haskell's head.

A scream was trapped in Haskell's throat. He threw up his arms to shield his face from shattering glass.

Haskell was stunned by sudden quiet. Slowly he lowered his arms. The curtains were blowing softly at the window. Gentle sounds returned, the chirrup of crickets, rustling of leaves. On the lawn were only shrubs and his grandmother's tulip tree in a circle of white stones, its long shadows trembling in the moonlight.

Haskell woke again to cool morning. He pulled on his jeans and slipped out to inspect the grass under his window. It was glistening with dew, and flattened here and there, but Haskell could find no certain hoof prints.

"I know what you want, Rondo!" Haskell said hoarsely. "You want me to tell Wendy I'm sorry! The hell with you! You shouldn't have thrown me off!" He shivered and giggled and shivered again. "Come back every night! I don't care!"

Alone at breakfast with his grandfather, he tried to be casual. Stirring his oatmeal, pouring on cream, he asked, "Granddad, did you hear anything else last night? I mean, besides Duchess?"

"No."

Haskell did not speak again until his oatmeal was nearly gone. "Granddad, do you believe in ghosts?"

"That depends on what you mean. I don't believe in spooks. But I know we can be haunted. A memory can haunt us, an idea, a phrase of music, a bad conscience."

Haskell looked at him warily. His grandfather was merely buttering toast and did not seem to have any special meaning.

"What could you do, then?"

"That depends on what was haunting you. If it was conscience, for instance, you could try to make amends."

Haskell had another question, that he did not ask. What if you were afraid?

His grandfather reached across the table to pat his hand. Haskell noticed how blue his eyes were. With his posture of a soldier on parade, he was quite handsome for an old guy.

Haskell heard Duchess all day, neighing and calling. Late in the afternoon, he went to the Bethune stable and watched until he was sure no one was there. He went in and found Duchess in her stall, head low, ears limp with exhaustion. She too was a bay and so much like Rondo, with the same blaze on her nose, that Haskell held back, expecting her to show Rondo's hatred of him.

Instead she perked up, put her ears forward and gave a welcoming whinny. He went to her.

"Hello, Duchess." When he felt her lips nuzzling his face, he burst into tears and threw his arms around her great, warm neck.

"I'm sorry about Rondo!" he whispered. "Please, please forgive me!" His own pain and loneliness, harbored for years, came flooding out, and he sobbed as he had not done since he was little. "I don't know how I got to be so rotten!" he said. "I don't want to be rotten. I want to be the way I was!"

He sensed that someone had come in. He broke away from Duchess.

It was Wendy. How much had she heard? He spun about, to dash through the back.

"Please don't run away!" Wendy called.

"I never run away!" Haskell cried. He was not going to apologize to her. If she had let him ride with a saddle and bridle, none of this would have happened. To his surprise, hot tears began spilling over his face again.

"Haskell, I wonder if you would groom Duchess today? I have so much to do in the tack room, I'm afraid I'll have to neglect her."

Haskell wiped his face.

"You know how, don't you?" Wendy asked.

"Of course I know how!"

"Duchess would be grateful. It would make her feel better." She added, "She seems to like you."

"Of course she likes me!"

Wendy led Duchess out of her stall and fastened her to cross ties. She showed Haskell the rack where her brushes and hoof picks were kept and went off to the tack room.

Haskell worked harder than he had since he had weeded in the garden with his grandmother. He gave the mare's coat a stiff brushing, combed her mane and tail, picked the stones and mud from her shoes and daubed oil on her hoofs. Duchess seemed to like the way he handled her and reached around now and then to nuzzle his hair. Haskell was shoveling out her stall when Wendy came back.

"She looks so proud of herself!" Wendy exclaimed. "I'm sure she thanks you very much, Haskell."

"She is welcome," Haskell said, gruffly. "Want me to feed her?"

"Yes, thank you! She gets a scoopful of grain in

her feed bin and fresh hay in her rack and clean water. Then would you put her back in her stall? Just fasten the stall guards and leave the gate open. That's how she likes it."

At the stable door, Wendy turned back. "Your grandfather said you might like to see Rondo's trophies."

Haskell followed her to the tack room. When she turned on the light, he was dazzled to see shelves of silver cups, trays, statuettes and bowls surrounding a great urn on a polished base.

"Did Rondo really win all these?"

"Most of them. Some belong to Duchess." Wendy took down a double-handled cup. "This is Rondo's last. He won it in a benefit show, just before you came." She put it in his hands and showed him the engraving of names and date.

"You may have it, if you like."

He shuffled. "Why?"

"I just thought you might like it."

What kind of crazy girl was she, anyway, Haskell wondered. Looking at her closely, he saw red welts under her eyes from crying.

"But why?" he asked again.

"To remember us by."

"If I wanted to remember, I wouldn't need this," he muttered. "But I'll keep it. I can put pencils in it."

She gave him a wry smile. As he left the stable, he called after her, "Could I sleep here with Duchess tonight?"

After dinner, Haskell moved the cot out of the tack room and set it up next to Duchess's stall. He folded Rondo's cooler for a pillow, pulled off his boots and lay down with his clothes on, wrapped in Rondo's blanket. The cot swayed and creaked when he moved and sagged when he lay still, but he had not expected to be comfortable, and did not plan to sleep.

He felt defiant of his fear, defiant of the hated person he had become. That person would take his punishment, whatever it might be. Let Rondo come and trample him!

In spite of all, he felt almost exultant, with Duchess close by, Duchess who trusted him and mistook him for a friend. He would be worthy of her friendship! He reached up to her muzzle. She brought her head close and sniffed him, lingering over Rondo's blanket.

They were quiet together for a long time. Moonlight streamed through the doorway, across Haskell's face. Crickets chirped in the boards. Duchess stamped, shifting her weight. Now and then she blew a gentle snort. Haskell began slipping off and had to struggle to stay awake.

Duchess raised her head sharply and gave a low whinny. Rising to his elbow, Haskell heard an answering nicker from afar and then hoofbeats coming up the road from the ring below, an uneven clopping, coming nearer and nearer.

A horse loomed in the doorway, blocking out the moon, throwing a long shadow. Duchess whinnied. The horse paced to her stall. They rubbed necks, with contented rumblings. The horse turned to Haskell and explored his hair and ears, the blanket, the cooler, sniffing and blowing. Haskell lay still, whispering through tears, "I'm sorry, Rondo. Please forgive me. I'll ask Wendy to forgive me. I'll ask everybody."

He tried to touch Rondo's muzzle, but he could not reach him. As in a dream, he could only move slowly, but his other senses were all working. He could see clearly in the moonlight, even the blaze on Rondo's nose. He could hear him, feel the warmth of his breath, smell his good horse odor.

At last Rondo seemed satisfied. With a whinny for Duchess, he backed, turned and clopped to the door, rump swaying, tail flicking, and passed out into the moonlight.

Haskell heard his hoofbeats receding for a long time. After a while he noticed that the horse was walking easily and evenly. The hoofbeats grew softer, and then there was nothing but the chirp of crickets, and Duchess stamping now and then and snorting gently.